Snapdragon

A Monster Popstar Romance

Sofia Rose

Other Books by Sofia

<u>SOFIA ROSE</u>

<u>Fortune Records Omegaverse:</u>

Snapdragon

Aster

Iris

Zinnia

Fritillaria

<u>Briar Hill Omegaverse:</u>

Touched & Tamed

<u>Whimsywood Tales:</u>

A Teacup for Trouble

<u>The Zodiac Society:</u>

Patreon exclusive, 13 novellas

A Note on Omegaverse

Before you begin, I wanted to take a moment to explain the version of omegaverse you'll find in this series.

Omegaverse is a romance subgenre that originated in fanfiction spaces and has since evolved into many different interpretations across books and authors. There is no single "correct" version. What follows is *my* take on omegaverse, and the rules that apply specifically to the world of the *Fortune Records Omegaverse*.

In this universe, society is divided between humans and monsters, who have historically lived apart. Because of this separation, humans do not grow up knowing about omegaverse dynamics. Human characters are unaware of secondary genders, heats, mating bonds, and related biology until they spend meaningful time with monsters. For humans, a dormant secondary gender is only triggered through meeting a monster mate.

Secondary Genders

In addition to primary sex, characters in this world have a secondary gender: **alpha** or **omega**. Any primary gender can be alphas or omegas. There are **no betas** in this universe.

Among monsters, secondary gender can be sensed instinctively. Humans do not have this ability in the same way, though some humans may experience a faint or inconsistent awareness of a mate. Monsters, particularly shifters, have heightened senses of smell, which makes their ability to scent secondary gender and mates far stronger and more reliable.

Omegas are not publicly labeled or categorized within human society.

Scent

Both alphas and omegas have distinct, unique scents, often influenced by personality, emotional state, and individual biology. A mate's scent is instinctively recognizable and often irresistible, creating a powerful pull between bonded partners.

When an omega becomes aroused, their scent sweetens, intensifying attraction and instinctual responses in nearby alphas. Scent plays a central role in attraction, bonding, and recognition throughout this world.

Heats and Instinct

Omegas experience heats, which are biological periods marked by heightened desire, sensitivity, and instinct. These urges often begin as an intensification of emotion and attraction, and can escalate into overwhelming instinct while in heat. Choice and consent still exist, but biology plays a powerful role in shaping how these experiences feel and unfold.

Mates and Bonds

Omegaverse bonds in this world are biological and deeply rooted in instinct. An omega will only ever be bonded to one alpha, and may also bond with additional omega mates within the same bond structure.

To complete a bond, two things must occur: a verbal acceptance of the bond, and a **claiming bite** from the alpha. The bite itself is pleasurable for the omega and marks the bond as fully formed. Until both acceptance and the bite occur, the bond remains incomplete.

Anatomy and Knotting

Male alphas in this universe have knots as part of their anatomy. A knot is an expanding ring of tissue around the base of an alpha's penis that swells during orgasm. This is a biological trait associated with mating and bonding.

Pack Structure

Pack dynamics in this world consist of one alpha with one or more omegas. These dynamics are instinctual rather than societal, and individual relationships may look very different depending on the characters involved.

This note is not meant to be exhaustive, but rather to offer grounding before you begin. As with all omegaverse stories, much of how these elements function is revealed through character experience, emotion, and connection.

Thank you for reading, and I hope you enjoy this world as much as I loved writing it.

Content Warning

The following book contains content that may be triggering for some readers. There are themes of segregation and manipulation.

Content includes: consensual non-consent, choking, breath play, primal play, chasing, a dominant/submissive relationship, somnophilia, omegaverse and knotting.

If you need any more information on any of the above, you can email me at sofiaroseauthor@gmail.com

Dedication

To anyone who has ever been in a relationship with a fic-
tional character.

I get it.

Chapter 1

"It *would* be good for your career, but I can see why you would also want to turn this down." I could hear the sigh coming from Frank, the line crackling with its intensity. "Actually, no. I have no idea of your thoughts on monsters, Flora. Heck, this is the height of unprofess ionalism..."

I cringe, trying to imagine Frank while he speaks. He's the perfect, clean cut professional. Every line is clear with him, and I always know what is expected from me.

We're both in new territory right now, though.

He's presented me with an interesting offer, to say the least. A luxury fashion house, Noma, has asked me to do a photo shoot. This would be a pretty big deal on any other day, but there's quite a significant caveat.

The shoot is a political stunt from Noma to appear more liberal and to cross sell their two markets. It's unusual for a business to be structured that way, a foot in both the human and the monster industries. Noma wants to do a photo shoot with a mixture of humans and monsters, featuring a whole host of us from different industries.

"I don't know, Frank." I tell him, honestly. "It's not that I personally have anything against monsters. But I'm afraid of what the backlash from this might be."

I was right. The tension between the two groups was high. I had never even met a monster.

"Can I take a bit of time to think about it?" I ask. This isn't a decision I should be making lightly. I fiddle with the elastic on my notebook while I wait on his response.

"I can try and get you an hour or two. I'll pretend I couldn't reach you or something." I relax a little, my shoulders brushing the smooth velvet of the booth behind me. "The shoot is planned for tomorrow though, so they're gonna push me."

I thank him, but he hangs up quickly. That's Frank, straight to the point and no frills.

I take a sip of my drink, the dainty tea cup shaking as I set it back down. I think I might need something stronger than matcha.

This wasn't what I expected from my morning visit to Rosie's café. I had been served my drink, the sun shining in the window and my songwriting notebook in front of me. That's when I got Frank's call.

I won't lie, there's definitely something to be said that Noma even knows who I am. It's still new to me that I'm recognized sometimes.

About a year ago, I went from singing at open mic nights, to selling out venues. It's all thanks to Frank. He spotted me, helped me finesse my skills, and got me a development deal with Fortune Records. It's been a whirlwind of a year since I met Frank, but I wouldn't change a thing.

I try to get back into the headspace I was in earlier, taking a deep breath and donning my signature smile.

OK, now I can get to thinking about this fashion shoot.

Monsters and humans do not mix. Ever.

My family has a pretty relaxed attitude, but I know that it's not the same for others. Humans are raised to hate monsters, we're told that they are abominations. That they shouldn't be allowed to share our spaces. Both groups feel the same way about the other, and stick to their own sides of the city.

I don't really know how I feel about it. I'm not the type of person to hate a stranger, never mind a whole group. Maybe doing this shoot could help with that though. I could mingle with some monsters, make a decision as to whether or not they are quite as terrible as we are all told to believe.

I contemplate why Noma is even doing all this. There are some political groups, usually younger college aged humans, who believe that we should all mix. They think that we would all be better for it.

It's become quite a heated topic of debate lately. I just wish I had been paying more attention to those conversations now.

My goal in life is to make music, but it's also more than that, it's to make people happy through my music.

"Are you alright, Flora?" I'm snapped out of my thoughts, Rosie leaning over me to set down my breakfast.

"Umm, yeah. Just fine, thanks." I pick up my cutlery to dig into my delicious looking avocado toast.

"That's a lie, if I ever heard one." She sits down on the chair across from me, flinging her dish towel over her shoulder. "I don't think I've ever seen you look so serious."

I set my cutlery back down, resting my chin on my hand. Rosie knows me well, too well sometimes.

She mirrors my body language, waiting for me to speak. "Fine. I'm not OK. I got the strangest phone call from Frank."

She leans forward slightly, practically drooling for the gossip.

"How do you feel about monsters?" I switch tactics.

That shocks her, "What? What's that got to do with Frank? Wait…" She wiggles her brows, "is Frank a monster, like in disguise?"

I blink at her slowly. Rosie is absolutely crazy, but that's why she's my best friend.

"You know," she continues, "I always thought he was keeping something secret. Ooh! This is hot, I suddenly find I'm feeling some attraction to Frank! Something about an older business exec does it for me, you know?"

"Eww, no. Absolutely not. Take that back," I pretend to throw up on my food.

Her bright blue eyes meet my golden brown, and we both burst into a fit of giggles.

"Stop," I squeal, wiping away my tears, "never, ever, ever talk about Frank again. You're officially cut off from this conversation. Go back to work."

I shoo her away with my hands and start to eat my food. At least avocado toast won't exactly go cold.

"Wait," she sniffles, earnestly trying to appear serious. "Tell me what it was."

I sigh, setting down the bite I was almost about to eat.

"There's been an offer for me to do a photo shoot with Noma tomorrow. Wait, no. No cheering yet. I'd have to be paired up with a monster for it."

Rosie's almost glee sobers instantly.

"Like, a real monster?" The light dimming in her voice a bit. "In person?"

"Yep." I say, popping the 'p' sound. "Plus, it's tomorrow. So I probably only have until I've finished my breakfast to make a decision on this."

"Well, obviously you have to do it." Rosie exclaims, throwing her arms up.

"What do you mean, obviously?"

"This kind of opportunity has even less of a chance than once in a lifetime. You will literally never be offered something like this again." She reaches across the table, gripping my hand in hers. "Come on! Where is my adventure loving, energy filled bestie hiding? You have been getting far too serious lately. Let loose, my love, go meet a monster!"

I anchor myself in her grasp and take a deep breath. She's right, of course. Rosie might be crazy, but she's usually right about these things. She hasn't led me wrong this far.

"You're right," I start.

"Always am!"

"Of course, you're always right, my magnanimous supreme reigner of all things correct." She takes a mock bow as she stands up. "I'll do it."

"That's my girl."

She heads back to work, helping out one of the new barista's with the cash register.

Rosie's café is stunning. She has created such a safe and inviting space here. It's truly one of my favorite places to be.

I finish my food, listening to the sounds of the café and watching the people on the street through the window.

Rosie's avocado toast is simply the best. I used to always have her make it for me when we were in college.

We've been friends since freshman year, when we got stuck in a triple dorm with the worst person to ever exist, Marilee.

Luckily, we made it through that tough time together. I would do it again to have Rosie in my life. After that year, we decided to move off campus, and we spent the next three years sharing the most run down little one bedroom apartment.

At least things had significantly improved for us since then. I now had a whole *two bedroom* apartment to myself, right down the street from Rosie's café.

Normally, I would spend the rest of my morning writing away in my notebook. I look at it on the table, the most obnoxious orange and pink glitter ombré. I love it.

But the vibes were not here this morning. A walk might make me feel a bit better.

One thing to do first though. I take out my phone, typing a text to Frank and letting him know I'll do the shoot.

I get up to go to the register, but the line is long so I peruse the little store section. This is probably my favorite part of the café. There are shelves of knick knacks and plants, plus a small little florist's station.

That's what catches my eye today, maybe fresh flowers will make me feel a little less unsettled.

I snatch up a pretty bouquet of pink and yellow snapdragons before checking out.

Waving goodbye to Rosie, I open the door to head outside when my phone dings. It's a text from Frank:

Good. My phone has been ringing off the hook. Call time is 7:30 am.

Chapter 2

I'm struggling to hold in the biggest yawn.

It turns out that a 7:30 am call time exceeds my usual limits. I can barely keep my eyes open with the weight of the fake lashes the makeup artist carefully applied.

She's adding the finishing touches to my look now, I realize, as I catch a glimpse of myself. It's weird to see the combination of full glam with my natural hair.

The hair stylist has added a soft wave to my long, golden locks. Normally, I wear wigs when doing anything singing related, but I guess I'm not promoting my music today. My onstage persona is a bit wild at times, and I favor colorful wigs and fun outfits.

My makeup is giving me a far different facial structure. I'm genuinely impressed by the cheekbones the artist has made appear on my round face. And is that a jawline I see?! Color me impressed.

Luckily, the makeup artist and hair stylist have been as sleepy as me, so we've mostly kept to a mutual silence.

The pair gently let me know that I'm ready and they will see me onset for touch ups.

Great, now I'm actually alone with my thoughts. I can feel the grogginess of the morning start to wear away and in its place is a bundle of nerves.

I startle as the door opens, a slip of a man barging in.

"Ah! Flora, perfect! Checking you're ready to go. I will be back around in a moment to take you to set."

He's gone in an instant.

Great. I wring my hands together, my anxiety rising. I didn't even get to ask anything about what's going to happen.

For a pretty sensitive situation, no one is really trying to prepare me at all. Frank doesn't start work this early, so I have no one that I can call.

What if it's on purpose? Maybe the monster is a beast and they don't want me to leave, so they're tricking me onto set so I can't say no.

They have me wearing a white, two piece set. A strip of a tube top and then a long and tight maxi skirt that shows the shape of my generous curves. I feel like a sacrificial lamb being brought to slaughter.

I take a deep breath, trying to calm my nerves. I hop out of the chair, needing to move. Pacing the room, I hum a nonsense tune to myself. It's a good distraction, as I find myself actually trying to compose something.

Inspired, I take out my phone and take a short recording of the melody.

I'm currently in the writing phase for my debut album. I've released an EP in the past, and a few singles too. But this is my first actual long form album.

I still get tingles when I think about the fact that this is my life now. My writing and recording schedule is mine to manage, and I get to work with Alex who I admire so dearly.

It's at that moment that the man comes back into the room, announcing that they are ready for me. I follow him down the hallway, feeling a flash of excitement along with my fear.

There aren't many people on set. The man who retrieved me and the photographer seem to be the only two humans at first glance.

Then there's the monsters. I can see two, and I pause, a stumble in my step for a moment.

The first is a tall, wiry gray-skinned man. When he shifts, I realize that he has a tail with a point at the end, too. He's dressed in a casual pair of jeans and a shirt, but they scream wealth.

The other is a beautiful wisp of a woman, with glorious translucent wings sprouting from her back. Her skin is tinged a pale blue and she wears a structured white pant suit. She flicks her long blue hair over a shoulder, looking at me with disapproval in her glare.

OK, then.

The photographer introduces himself as Benedict. I've heard of his work before and I compliment him on a recent magazine shoot he did.

Benedict bows his head lightly, "I didn't expect you to be familiar with my work. My humblest gratitude, my dear."

A low vibration begins behind me, or at least I think that's what it is. Turning to see, I am greeted with a wide expanse of chest, clad in a loose white shirt. I need to look *up* to see this person.

It's him that's making the noise, almost like a growl of sorts. He doesn't look impressed, to say the least.

"Flora, my dear," the growl becomes more intense, "this is your co-star for the day. Please let me introduce Sebastian Orville and his team. Sebastian, this is Florence Augustine."

I use the time Benedict is speaking to look at Sebastian. He is *large*. Deep brown skin, shoulder length black hair hanging loose around a face framed with structure. This man did not need the contouring that I did.

His eyes are a bright, glowing green, his pupils slit like a cat. If not for his size, the true giveaway that this is not a human is the scales. Patches of varying sizes stand out beneath the shirt, almost looking like tears across his skin. They're black with a sheen of the same green as his eyes, he even has some on those high cheekbones.

A hand gently prods my elbow, and I cringe, realizing I have been staring too long. Benedict is looking at me expectantly.

"Sorry," I falter over my words, "I think I missed what you said."

"No worries, I was directing you to move forward here." He guides me to my marker.

Benedict spends a bit of time figuring out how best to work with the height difference between Sebastian and I.

I'm not a small woman, I am 5'7" and I'm not skinny by any means. But Sebastian dwarfs me. I had a friend in college that was 6'3" and even he would look short compared to Sebastian.

I watch as he is directed by Benedict to stand a good bit behind me.

"I will use forced perspective, I think." He mutters to himself. I smile and gently giggle at his utter lack of preparation. I glance at Sebastian to share my smile and lighten the mood, also just to look at him more.

He catches my glance and immediately looks away, his strong brows furrowing. He scowls at the gray-skinned man, who seems to sneer in response.

The rest of the shoot goes pretty much the same way. We're not directed to actively look at one another at any point. Anytime I actually do look his way, he is pointedly *not* looking at me.

I don't let my disappointment show on my face, or at least I try not to. Now that I'm here, I'm not sure what I expected from the monsters. I mean, they seem pretty normal, if a little rude and grumpy. But I'm not exactly getting that 'once in a million lifetimes' excitement level that I was expecting.

That being said, I am not letting my guard down for one second. I'm painfully aware that I have my back to a well-honed killing machine. Sebastian could definitely take me in a fight. I wouldn't stand a chance. Let's be real, there wouldn't even be a fight.

My breath quickens at the thought, and I feel a pulse of heat go straight to my core.

Nope. Not now, absolutely not. I'm not letting my guard down, remember?!

I can't help but look back at Sebastian again. He's not looking away this time. Our gazes meet for a moment and there is an intensity there that I can't quite seem to figure out. A muscle ticks in his jaw and I don't know why that has suddenly become an incredibly attractive thing for a person to do.

"That's a wrap!" Benedict calls out. "Great work, both of—" He is cut off as Sebastian storms out of the room, no attempt at any kind of subtlety. The two other monsters follow suit and the door slams loudly behind them.

I'm startled right out of my strange thoughts. Fuck, what is wrong with me?!

"Thank you, my dear. You did lovely." Benedict pats my shoulder. "I wish this could have been a nicer experience, but we made do."

Plastering a smile on my face, I shake his hand. "It was a pleasure to work with you, Benedict. Perhaps we will do so again in the future."

With that, I turn and leave the set quickly. I race back down the hall to my dressing room, my fingers trembling as I open the door.

My wardrobe assistant is inside, ready to take my clothes back and I nearly sob right in her face. I need some time alone right now to process. I don't get it, it's not like anything particularly dramatic happened. My body is telling me a different story though, as I try to hold still through my tremors.

I feel wrong. Like a part of me is missing.

Chapter 3

I wake up to sunlight pouring into my room. It shines right onto my bed and makes it so warm and cozy.

I don't understand people who like blackout blinds. I love it when a space feels light and airy. Waking up before my alarm to sunshine is so simple and yet it has to be up there with my favorite feelings.

I turn over and grab my phone, snuggling up in my lavender colored sheets to bask in the warmth while I scroll. The algorithm isn't cutting it this morning though. So I get up, slipping on a pair of cozy wool thigh-highs. I also grab an oversized cardigan to throw on over my silky sleep set.

Softly padding into my little kitchen, I flick on the switch to the pastel green coffee machine. I grab my favorite daisy print mug and set it under the spout. The beautiful snapdragons I bought two days ago are blooming nicely and I bend over to smell them.

This coffee machine was one of my first big purchases when I started to make a little money. It's still by far one of my best. It's a high tech bean to cup that cleans itself when it's done. What more could a girl ask for?

I open my pantry cupboard, realizing that I need to buy groceries. After I root around for a bit, I find a questionable peanut butter breakfast bar. I guess that will have to do.

Listening to a vinyl could be nice. I look through my collection, picking out the soothing sounds of Clarissa Raye. Only my hardcore fans would understand the influence that she has on my music. I have a beautiful special edition of her first album, and that's what I decide to put on.

I pour the last drops of the creamer into my mug, grab that and my bar, and make my way out to my balcony. Leaving the door to the balcony open so I can hear Clarissa, I curl up on my little loveseat.

Once I am still for a moment, the previous day replays in my mind. I can't ignore the stream of thoughts pouring through me.

Sebastian Orville is a prime, grade A asshole.

My skin crawls just thinking about his behavior yesterday. Whether or not he wanted to be there, he could have at least *tried* to be polite!

And what was with the weird growling? I could have let that slide as a weird cultural difference if it weren't for everything else.

Now that I think of it, I don't even think I heard any of the three monsters speak. What? Was I too beneath them for my ears to be blessed by the great sounds of their voices? Fuck that. Who the fuck does a full photo shoot without even speaking?

I rip open the wrapper to my breakfast bar and take a bite, my teeth grinding furiously on the poor peanuts. My mug is trembling under my tight grip.

OK, take a deep breath, Flora. Life is good. You have cozy knits, dreamy music, and comforting coffee. All is good with the world.

It's not long before my thoughts stray back to Sebastian though. I've never felt so small before in my life. That was kind of nice at least.

I feel like I didn't get a good look at his hands, but I bet they were huge. He could probably circle my neck with one of those hands... it doesn't matter. I am never going to see him again anyway.

Thankfully, my thoughts are saved by the buzzing of my phone on the kitchen counter. I go back inside, stopping my vinyl and grabbing the offending device.

"Frank? I thought you promised me a day off after yesterday?" I whine, answering the phone.

"I did, I know. Normally I would stick to that, but things have been..." I plop onto my couch, waiting for him to continue. "How did things go at the photo shoot yesterday? Was the other side's team agreeable?"

That was a switch in tactic if I ever heard one. The thing with Frank is, I know that he has my best interests at heart, for the most part. The best thing is to humor him.

"It was weird, to be honest." Stroking the fur on the throw draped over my couch, I continue. "They didn't do anything bad, I guess. But they also didn't do anything good either. There were three of them and not a single one spoke a word while I was in the room."

"I don't get it then," he says. "The artist's manager said he was blown away by your chemistry... The label is in uproar as we speak. Karl, the manager, has been telling everyone he can that you and the artist..."

Karl must have been the gray-skinned man then.

"*Sebastian*," I fill in for him, unable to keep the disdain from my voice.

"Yes, Sebastian... Well, Karl says that you two hit it off."

What?! What room was Karl even standing in? Did his super secret monster powers allow him to travel to a different dimension or something?

"The label has been looking to follow in Noma's footsteps. To do a big crossover between monsters and humans as well, but they haven't had a good idea on how to do it."

"I'm not sure what that's got to do with us," I quip, a warning in my voice.

"Well... look, Flora. This Karl guy has been going at it, and the label believes that they've found their golden ticket, as it were."

I'm glad I'm sitting, the pastel hues of my living space blurring together as the room spins.

"No." I tell him, brokering no argument. That doesn't stop him though.

"All it would be is a few dates. A publicity stunt. Something the label can control without actively looking like they're contributing to it. We'll find a way to break it off at that point and then we can move on with our lives."

I sigh. "What do you know about him? Sebastian, I mean."

"He's apparently a very big name in the monster music industry. He's on his fifth album, got a few platinum records." Well that explains his attitude then.

"What about *him*, though?" I push on. "What kind of monster is he?"

"Oh, um, I didn't think to ask."

"What? So I'm just supposed to publicly associate myself with him, and you didn't think to ask?!" I am struggling to calm my breathing now, my foot tapping on the rug.

"I'll find out, don't worry. We'll get through this together."

"You won't have to do anything," I counter. "I'm the one who will have to be near him, Frank. This isn't what I signed up for when we met. I just want to make my music and perform, that's all."

"Don't be naive, Flora. Sometimes record labels will have their artists do stunts like this for PR. It happens all the time, it's part of the job." I can hear the exasperation in his voice.

"But not with monsters!" I had expected something like this to happen at some point, but with an actor or something. A *human* actor.

"I know, you're right. I'm being insensitive. This is a big ask." At least he was finally seeing reason. "Think about it, OK? I won't rush you on this one like the photo shoot."

"Lucky me." I say, hanging up.

I toss my phone on the couch, heading back out to the balcony to finish my coffee. Now I needed to come up with a good plan to get out of this.

Chapter 4

I hold the door for a man with a takeout bag and a tray of smoothies before I can actually make it into Rosie's café. I usually avoid the busy lunch rush, choosing to grab a late breakfast most days.

There's a hectic energy surrounding Rosie as she flits from table to table. I grab a seat tucked away in the back to try and avoid the crowd.

I hadn't planned on coming here today, I had wanted to spend the day in solitude. But after that call with Frank, I needed my best friend. Not that she is going to have any time for me right at this moment, which is fine. I can have lunch while I wait for her to be free.

I order a Buddha bowl from Farrow when she swings by, her bubblegum pink hair blending in perfectly with the surrounds.

My phone dings with a text from Frank:

He's a dragon shifter. That's all I can get.

A d*ragon shifter*?! He can't mean... does he... *become* a dragon?

I think back to yesterday again, imagining his form. He did have those scales, and he was huge. I can't imagine how the whole shifting thing would work though.

Intrigued, I pull out laptop from my tote bag. I've never even tried to search much about monsters online before. Where do I even start?

"Dragon shifters," I mutter each syllable softly as I type it into the search bar. I get a pop up immediately, warning me that there is sensitive content. I hesitate, before clicking through to see the results.

The first result is *All You Need To Know About Dragon Shifters*, so I click through. I barely scan the first few sentences before I realize that this is in fact very sensitive content. Whoever wrote this blog post is *sexually* interested in dragon shifters.

I click back before I can read too much. I scroll through the next few results before finding an excerpt from an academic text. Perfect, this is more what I'm looking for.

The contents within may not be factually correct, as much evidence is based on unverifiable eye-witness accounts.

Yikes. I guess monsters do really keep information about themselves under lock and key. I start to read through the reports, but it's all conflicting information. One human man claims that he saw a dragon breath fire, another woman claims ice. There's a lot of back and forth as to whether they even have a humanoid form or not.

We know the truth about that, at least.

I don't come away from the article with any more information than before, and it's incredibly frustrating.

A cup of tea is set down next to my laptop.

"Oh, but I didn't order—" I say, looking up to find Rosie.

"No," she agrees. "But you looked like you needed it. I'll be around to chat once this dies down a bit." She gestures around herself as if I hadn't already noticed the bustling café.

"Thank you," I call after her as she gets back to work.

I take a sip of my tea, the temperature perfect. It tastes like her calming chamomile blend.

Sighing, I lean back into the velvet cushions, contemplating the life choices that led me here.

I came here to talk to Rosie about the PR plans from the label, but I realize now that I can't tell her. The label is most definitely going to make me sign a non-disclosure agreement, listing that I can't tell anyone that it's a PR stunt.

Is this really what I want for myself?

I wanted to share my music with people who it could bring joy to. It's probably because I haven't released new music in a few months, but I'm feeling a bit disconnected from my audience already. Never mind that the label is now concocting this scheme.

I force down a gulp of tea and then take a deep breath. Maybe I need to do a dance class. I text Daisy and Cleo, my backup dancers, to see if they're free.

Yeah, babe. We can do tomorrow morning?

Daisy is the one to text back, usually one of the pair will text back for them both. It's not as soon as I would like, but tomorrow will do. I confirm that I'll join.

Farrow brings along my Buddha bowl and I almost drool at the sight. If anything, I at least always have food as a comfort. Rosie's signature Buddha bowl is delicious.

It's a delectable mix of falafel, avocado, spinach, edamame, shredded carrot, topped with pomegranate seeds and a tahini dressing. Also known as heaven.

I shut my laptop, deciding to focus on my food and my surroundings. I have a feeling that I could keep searching on there forever and not be any closer to the truth.

I finish my food and order a hazelnut latte. I might as well have more caffeine to get me through this day. I'm not sure what to do at this point. Do I go for the PR stunt, or say no? *Can* I say no?

Sure, Frank has said he will give me the time, but I know that's because he expects me to say yes at the end of it. My development deal will finish in a couple months, and if the label isn't happy with me they will drop me. I'm sure of it.

It's not that my music has been doing poorly, but they won't want someone on their books that they can't manipulate.

This is a disaster.

It takes a while, but eventually Rosie is able to take the seat across from me.

"Tell me everything!"

"It was strange, Rosie. They were kind of scary, but mostly just... aloof?" Her expression falls and I know she was expecting something juicier. "I kind of regret doing it to be honest. They didn't speak to me at all. We got the pictures taken and then they left."

Rosie looks crestfallen, her brows drawing close together and she worries at her lip.

"I'm sorry, Flo. I thought it would have been super fun and exciting."

I grab her hand across the table. "I know, it's totally not your fault. How would you have known anyway? Don't be so hard on yourself."

We sit in silence for a moment. The café has emptied out significantly, the deafening noise from earlier quietening down to a lull.

"You know what we need?" Rosie quips with a gleam in her eye. "A night out!"

"Ugh, you are so right!" I tell her. "When?"

"Why not tonight? I can pick you up in an Uber this evening. We try that new club on 4th Street that we've been meaning to go to."

This is exactly what I need. A night of dancing, letting go, and forgetting about life.

Chapter 5

My dress is a little itchy, the gold sequins digging in where it ends at my thigh. My shapewear is protecting me up until that point at least. Being a curvy girl is all fun and games until you have to fold up into the tiny back seat of an Uber in a tight, sequined dress.

I spent the full afternoon in the café researching every bit of information that I could find on dragon shifters. I didn't learn anything concrete.

Not. A. Single. Thing.

It seemed like every piece of information was contradicted by another. I even ended up on *those* websites, the ones that were very interested in dragon shifters, indeed.

I don't think I realized quite so many different anatomies could exist, sexually I mean.

After that, I went home and got ready. I may have already downed a few shots of questionable whiskey that I found in the back of my cupboard before going down to meet Rosie in the Uber.

I rub at my chest now, feeling the burn there still. That whiskey had been opened a while. I'm sure I've already somehow poisoned myself.

I look over at Rosie, who looks stunning, as always. She's wearing a cobalt blue slip dress that makes her bright blue eyes sing. Her chocolate brown hair is softly waved and pinned back to hang over one shoulder.

"You look stunning," I tell her. "If I were a man, I would be drooling over you right now."

"What if you were a monster?" she gives me her signature brow wiggle that she does when she's teasing.

"Stop!" I exclaim. "We're done talking about monsters. I'm so over them right now."

"Bah! Don't think I didn't see you on those monster lover sites earlier."

I blush, sometimes Rosie observes a lot more than you think. I should have been more discreet.

"What were they like, anyway?" she continues, missing my embarrassment entirely. "What kind of monster was he? Your co-star?"

"Well I couldn't tell at the time, but Frank got the info. He's a *dragon shifter...*"

"A *what*?!"

"I know! That's what I was researching all day today. But before you ask, I literally know nothing. I couldn't find anything online."

I glance up at that moment, catching the disapproving gaze of the Uber driver in his rear view mirror. The judgment in his eyes sobering up all of the whiskey I drank earlier. He looks *disgusted*, like I am a piece of gum he found on his shoe.

Luckily, the car pulls to a stop as we arrive at the club. I hop out quickly and wait for Rosie on the pavement.

The line to the club is massive, at least fifty people deep. It's going to take us ages to get in.

"Ugh," Rosie states, "remind me why I was all excited to go to a new club, again? Everyone and their mother is here!"

"Should we go somewhere else, maybe?" I suggest. We are still standing near the entrance, contemplating walking down to the end of the line.

A group walks by us, heading straight for the door and skipping the line altogether. The bouncer easily lets them through.

"Either get in line or move along ladies!" The other bouncer keeping the line in check shouts to us.

"She's with me." A deep voice calls out, and I turn to see a stunning man with golden hair and tan skin. He's with the group that were just let through. We make eye contact as he continues, "her friend too."

Rosie whistles softly, before pulling me by the elbow and meeting the golden boy at the door.

He grins at me, one dimple showing on his cheek as he gestures for us to follow him. I turn back to look at Rosie and she has a grin plastered on her face.

"You're that singer, right? Usually has funny colored hair?" Golden boy's deep timbre calls out from ahead.

"Yeah that's me," he stops, turning to shake my hand. The warmth of his closeness is intoxicating. I can definitely feel that whiskey kicking in for real now.

"I'm Cian," he says, leaning forward and getting more in my space. Oh, this man is into me. Thank goodness, I need a good sexy night to clear my head from everything going on.

"Flora," I say, a little breathless. "And that's Rosie."

He turns to look at her, "It's a *pleasure*."

His hand moves to my lower back as he guides us for-ward, the pulsing sound of the club music coming from down the hall.

"I couldn't allow two beautiful ladies to be left standing out in the cold." He grins at me, waiting for the reaction to his compliment. I smile up at him and flutter my lashes a little. "Would you like to join my friends and I for the evening? We have a private booth, that's where I'm going right now."

"Hmm..." I say, pretending to think about it. "What do you think, Rosie?"

She twirls a flirty piece of her hair around a finger, "I guess a booth could be nice."

"Then it's settled."

He keeps his hand on my back as we head down to meet his friends.

***

His friends are fun. Cian is fun, actually.

His lighthearted and playful flirting is exactly what I needed. He twirls me around on the dance floor, the gold-en sequins of my dress changing colors with the lights.

I've consumed a few more drinks now, the champagne and cocktails flowing at Cian's booth. From what I've gathered so far, either Cian's or someone else's Dad is important in the government or something like that. So I think they get special treatment, or they're super rich. Probably both.

I don't mind why we're getting it, as long as it keeps coming and Cian's warm body still feels as good against mine. He spins me around again, before pulling my back tight against his front. His arms wrap around me and hold me there as we sway to the music.

I feel Cian's hands caress my waist before moving down to grip my hips. He tugs me closer against him, his hard cock pressing into my back.

I groan, tipping my head back and grinding against him. A warmth is pooling in my pussy and I make the decision to go home with Cian tonight. His cock feels so good pressed against me.

I twist in his grip and press my stomach against him. Looking up, I give him my best bedroom eyes, our dancing long forgotten.

His pale blue eyes find mine and I stretch up on my toes. I want him to kiss me, and I am giving him every signal that I can think of.

He leans down, his face close to mine. I can smell the alcohol on his breath, his hands gripping me tighter against him.

He bends further and I hold in a disappointed sound when he moves to the side. He runs his nose against my neck before speaking in my ear.

"I would love to kiss you right now, Flora." He grinds against me again, a little thrust involved this time and it is so difficult to hold in my moan. "But I can't be seen doing much more in public.... my father would have my head."

His hand distracts me from his words, leaving tingles behind as he runs it up and down my back. "I'm sure you have to worry about that too? With your singing?"

Hmm...? Oh, yes. Conversation. I'm having a conversation.

"Yeah," I sigh. "I guess I *am* pretty important too."

I giggle at my own joke, but he's taking me so seriously. It's kind of adorable, actually.

"How about we hang out at the table a bit more? I'm not going to be able to control myself if we keep dancing like this..."

I let him take my hand, pulling me along behind him. I hold in a disappointed sigh. This was a bust. Maybe he might still want to go home with me, though.

But when we get to the table, he tells me he's going to the bathroom and deposits me with Rosie.

"That was weird," I tell her. "I think he is worried about publicity or something, I don't know. All I know is that asshole got me super horny and then fucked off."

"Fuck him!" she declares, taking a gulp of her drink. "Here," she says, passing me a cocktail, "drink up. You'll feel better."

I try to have some fun with Rosie, but I need more alcohol to kick into my system right now.

I take my phone out of my purse to check it. So many emails have come through since I left my apartment earlier this evening.

Scrolling through the subjects, I stop when I see an email from Noma with the subject:

Photos for approval.

It's an email to my team that I'm copied on. I click through immediately, eager to see the shots. I wasn't joking when I said I liked Benedict's work, and I was curious as to how I would look in the photos.

"The photos are here," I nervously tell Rosie.

"Ooh, lemme see!" she goes to grab my phone.

"Wait, I haven't looked at them yet. Here, look with me."

We both lean over my phone as I click through. The first few images are only me, and wow, I actually look good in them. I'm not always great at looking at photos of myself, but these I could get on board with.

When I click to the next photo, it's me and Sebastian. Rosie snatches the phone out of my hand. "You didn't tell me he was that hot!" she exclaims. "We need to talk about when I ask you what happened and you say nothing. Because, bitch, this man is *fine!* I mean, look at those scales, and he's huge!"

"I know," I admit. "And that's not even our real height difference... they had me stand way in front of him to make the perspective better."

Her jaw literally drops. Then she leans back over the phone to look again.

"Umm, can I actually see the photo, Ro? You know, seeing as I'm in it."

She flips the phone around so it's facing me. "You both look so good together. Like, your chemistry is *palpable.*"

Rosie's not wrong. Sebastian's dark skin and hair contrast against my tan skin and honey blond. He's looking at me so intensely. I hadn't seen that side of him at all when we were taking the photos. He looks magnificent, and I find myself forgetting all about Cian.

Cian doesn't want me to forget him that easily though. Arms wrap around me from behind, "Hey baby, why don't we get out of—"

His words are quickly followed by a sound of pure and raw disgust. "Ugh! Why are you in a photo with that *abomination*?!"

He pulls away from me as I turn to look at him. I can see it in his eyes, the moment his personality switches, and a petulant little boy comes out.

"I can explain—" I start.

"Get out of our booth. Now." He gestures to the dance floor.

I stand still, as does Rosie, we're both in shock at his quick reaction.

"I said, get out of our booth." His voice raises to a shout, "you filthy monster fucking slut!"

Luckily, Rosie's brain is working better than mine, clearly sensing the danger here. She grabs our things and pulls us away before he can escalate things further. She drags me towards the exit, pausing in the hallway by the door to look behind us.

When we get outside, she wraps my jacket around my shoulders, pulling me out of the way and ordering us an Uber.

"It's OK, honey." She rubs my back. "Better you find out now that he's clearly a psycho."

It doesn't take long for the Uber to arrive. She guides me into my seat and buckles me in.

"You OK?" she asks, patting my cheek.

I take a second before answering.

"Yeah..." my mind drifts away for a moment, seeing the hate in Cian's eyes again. "Yes. Sorry, I'm in shock."

I smile at her, "I'm good. I was surprised, that's all. Thanks for getting us out of there."

I realize she's holding my hand, and I squeeze her fingers once.

"OK. But I'm coming home with you." She declares.

"No, you don't have to. I swear I'm fine." I let go of her hand. "Besides, I have an early start tomorrow."

***

I'm trembling by the time I get home and shut the door behind me.

I sink to the floor, my head in my hands as I begin to sob. My chest constricts with heaving breaths and all I can do is lean into it.

I was just so shocked by Cian's reaction. People don't like monsters, I get that. But to have such a visceral response. The reason had to run so much deeper, right? He had said that his father was important… maybe he was indoctrinated since birth into a crazy family. But still, how could someone hate with so much fire? Why did he care?

I think back to the Uber driver on the way to the club too. He was the same.

Were the monsters that I met particularly kind? No. But did they deserve this kind of reaction? I don't think so. They may have been rude, but no one actually did anything to me. They could have, too. There was hardly any security in the studio. If they were all so bad, they would have taken advantage somehow, I'm sure of it.

Pulling out my phone, I look at the photos of me and Sebastian properly.

He really is looking at me like he cares. It's such a juxtaposition to what I experienced in person. I wonder if I was silently judging them with my own preconceived notions. Maybe I was no better than Cian, or the Uber driver.

I realize what I need to do.

I can't sit here and judge anyone else for their reactions. Not when I have an opportunity to change things. I can show people that a human and a monster can be friends. That they can go on dates. That they can interact without the world imploding.

I open up my text chain with Frank, the words 'dragon shifter' seeming to jump out of the screen at me.

My fingers hover over the keys. Am I really going to do this? I don't know anything about monsters, but I'm smart enough to know that a dragon sounds pretty dangerous.

I'm shaking, and I have to delete and retype my message twice before hitting send.

Two words. Two simple words staring back at me.

I'm in.

Chapter 6

I know things have been bad lately, but resorting to self harm isn't the answer.

Clearly, I have turned to self harm though. Because there is no other explanation for being in a dance studio the morning after a night at the club. So self harm it is. I wonder if I need therapy.

My head is pounding, and it's only made worse by Cleo patting me on the back.

"Wake up, buttercup." Her and Daisy share a giggle at my despair.

I'm currently bent at the waist, panting heavily. The room spins a little as I straighten and take a sip of my water. We've only finished warm ups, and I feel like we have been dancing for days. I catch a glimpse of myself in the mirror and look away as quickly, I don't need to see that.

Daisy and Cleo are two of my backup dancers on stage, that's how we met. Being on tour grows strong bonds, and so I do a few dance classes with them every week. It helps me to stay in shape, and it's worth it for the gossiping we do.

"So... we saw a little sneak peek on Noma's socials this morning!" Although, it appears that I am the topic of gossip this morning. "Tell us everything."

"Oh," I reply to Cleo. "I didn't see that they had posted anything. I literally just rolled out of bed and into my car this morning."

"Here, look!" Daisy holds out her phone to me.

Noma shared a sneak peek, alright. It's individual head-shots for now, nothing with the couples. I must still be drunk because I can hear myself telling them that there were couple shots too.

"Which one?"

I point to the smoldering photo of Sebastian.

"I can't really see him properly..." Cleo sighs.

"Fine." I tell them, begrudgingly. "I have the full photos."

I pull out my phone and show them both the shots with Sebastian.

"He's a hunk!" Daisy exclaims, receiving a few strange looks from other girls in the class.

"OMG, yes!" Cleo agrees. "I'd take a piece of that any day. And you guys look so good together…"

I blush as Daisy nods vigorously.

"Are you into him?" she asks.

"Ladies! Enough chatting, let's get started on this combination." Our instructor calls out, saving me from responding.

Chapter 7

I'm seeing him again. *Sebastian.*

Everything moved so quickly.

I had three missed calls from Frank by the time I finished the dance class. My thighs burned and all I wanted was to go home and get back into bed. It strikes me that Frank would be pissed if I called *him* this early in the morning.

I waddled to my car and called him back. Frank outlined that my first appearance with Sebastian was *tonight*. We would be attending an awards show for the film industry as guests. And yes, there would be a red carpet.

So here I am, dressed up to the nines and waiting in my apartment building's lobby for a car to pick me up.

The label sent me a stunning dress, at least. I'm artfully draped in olive green satin, the corseted waist meeting loose off the shoulder drapes. It flows from the waist, with a high slit up one thigh. It feels luxurious, the buttery soft fabric definitely being an apology from the label for this.

My skin glows. The team that came to get me ready scrubbed and polished me, before dousing me in a fig-scented glittery oil.

I stayed with my natural hair again. I thought that my wigs wouldn't have met the level of class that we were aiming for with this look. Although, several sets of extensions were currently clipped in tightly to my head.

I catch a glimpse of a sleek black limo pulling up through my peripheral. Oh, the label certainly did not spare any expense.

I leave them waiting there for a moment, my nerves getting the better of me. I'm not sure if Sebastian would be in the car or not, and I don't know what I will say if he is.

I steal myself and take a deep breath. I can do this.

Keeping my head high and my shoulders back, I leave the building as the driver comes out to open my door.

I'm presented with two things when I enter the car. Firstly, Sebastian looked good before, but the black tux gives him a level of sophistication that I can't even begin to comprehend. Secondly, we're not alone.

There is a beautiful, delicate creature here. She is thin and willowy, with a set of horns growing out of the front of her head. They're framed by a pair of down-turned ears, with soft tufting fur.

"Hi!" I say to her in my cheeriest voice. "I'm Flora, it's lovely to meet you."

She takes my outstretched hand and gives me a warm, glowing smile. "Hi, Flora. I'm Matilda. I'll be assisting you and Sebastian this evening." Her cheeriness takes me off guard. I guess not all monsters are grumps. She's bubbly in the way that an intern in their first job would be. It's adorable, and I warm to her immediately.

"Hi Sebastian," I speak towards him now. "It's so nice to see you again."

He barely looks at me, grunts, and then pointedly stares out the window.

Unfortunately, that is how most of the journey goes. Sebastian, sitting as far away from me as possible. Matilda looking painfully awkward between us. I've noticed that instead of feet, she has *hooves*.

I see her looking nervously between us now. Her mouth opens as if to speak a couple times, and it's hard to watch.

"Is there anything you need for us to do during the journey?" I ask her, trying to put her out of her misery.

"Yes!" She looks relieved, the poor thing. "Umm... well... the label asked me to take a photo of you for your socials. In the car I mean."

She looks between us both. "They've given me instructions on how it should look, too."

Sebastian makes no attempt to move, or even acknowledge poor Matilda. So I stand up as much as I can and brush myself off.

"I presume you want us together?" I ask her.

"Yes, please. If you wouldn't mind sitting next to Sebastian." I move closer and sit next to him. We're not touching, but I can feel the heat emanating from him.

"If you could lounge back, Sebastian. Drape your arm across the seat behind Flora." She instructs, and he does as he is told, surprisingly. I want to lean into his warmth and it's taking everything I have not to.

"Perfect. Now, Flora, could you scooch a little closer?" I do so, pressing my side against him fully. I can feel him everywhere, even in the places we're not touching.

"Turn in to face him fully," I angle myself more towards him. "That's it. And now put your hand on his cheek."

Matilda moves to guide me into place, and Sebastian's head whips around to glare at her, a short rumble in his chest. Her hand freezes mid way, before she pulls it away altogether. What the fuck? All I can gather from that is that he doesn't want her to touch me? What, did he think that being human was contagious?

I barely remember my instruction and move my hand up to rest on the side of his face. My thumb brushes against the patch of scales there, the texture smoother than I expected. They are more so firm and soft rather than hard or rough.

"Stretch your arm out, as if you're taking the photo." She instructs Sebastian once my hand is in place. I realize now that they want it to look like he's taking a selfie while I'm nearly draped over his lap.

His whole presence is firm, and hot, and *big*. I can feel my nipples hardening and I am so grateful for the thick panels of this corset.

"Can you both look at each other please?"

I shift my view up, trying to avoid his eyes. My hand looks so small against his cheek. I may try, but they can't be avoided forever. One small glance and my eyes are locked onto his. I didn't get to look at his eyes properly the first time we met. Now I have the chance to study them in detail. I hear Matilda working away with her photo taking, but I hardly notice. His eyes glow, but the bright green isn't as one dimensional as I first thought. There are flecks of so many shades of green in there too. His slit pupils don't throw me off kilter this time either, and I can appreciate the beauty in them now.

Matilda sighs, "Can you smile, Flora?"

I instantly plaster an open-mouthed smile on my face, like I'm laughing at something funny Sebastian said. I follow directions pretty easily, sometimes I just do it without thinking. This was one of those times.

"Perfect! That's it. I'm going to send that to you now, Sebastian, and you can post it to your socials." I'm kicked right out of my daydream, straight into reality as Sebastian pulls away from me.

"Keep that up on the red carpet, you two."

The car pulls to a stop and I can hear the uproar of a crowd outside. I blink slowly, trying to regain my composure. I don't get that chance though. Sebastian rises, and the door is opened.

I'm surprised at how his demeanor changes. He gives me a charming smile, holding out his hand to me. I let him guide me out of the car and am shocked further when his hand caresses my lower back.

"Don't forget to smile, sunshine." His deep voice carries to me on a whisper. I need to hold in a whimper at the sound, my thighs clenching together as I put on my best smile.

The camera flashes are overwhelming as I try to look up at him like I actually want to be here. Everyone else arriving has been abandoned by the press, who's only focus is now on Sebastian and I. It's overwhelming. Admittedly, the only thing grounding me in this moment is Sebastian's hand on my back, guiding me forward and to the event.

The staff don't know what to do with us.

I had been so nervous and overwhelmed since this was sprung on me earlier today, that I hadn't really thought about the logistics. It seems the label hadn't either. In fact, I don't think anyone at the event knew that we would be arriving together.

This isn't done. Monsters and humans don't mix like this. There's a standard set of rules for when events like these occur. Those rules include two different red carpets, one for the humans and one for the monsters.

The staff for the event are still looking at us with confusion as we make our way through the paparazzi.

"We can go to the monster side," I suggest to Sebastian. We've lost Matilda in the commotion already.

"No." He grunts. "I will go with you to the humans. It's much safer."

That's all he says to me as he guides me forward. He instructs the staff in clipped tones and they all bend over themselves to help us.

We are directed to stand in line now, a brief reprieve from the press ensuing. Red carpets still surprise me. I used to see the photos in magazines and online, and think that it looked so glamorous and fun. In reality? It was just a lot of famous people, all lined up together like cattle, waiting to get their picture taken to be allowed inside.

The other humans in line with us are being polite, but I can see their uncertainty as they glance up at Sebastian. They're just being well behaved because of all the cameras around.

His hand remains firmly planted on my lower back, his thumb absentmindedly stroking me there as we wait. I sigh, comforted by the movement.

"Thank you," I tell him. "That could have been much worse and taken a lot longer."

He grunts in response. I sigh for a different reason this time. I thought he would be more vocal now that we were alone.

"Not much of a talker, are you?" I look up at him, blown away again by how attractive he looks in this tux. Especially now that he was standing.

He doesn't respond, looking at me intensely. I spot the moment when his eyes drift lower, taking in my breasts first, and then my entire form. I want to say something, but I don't know what. Sebastian looks like he wants to eat me, and I'm not so sure I would try to stop him.

We're ushered forward by a staff member. It's time for us to take to the carpet. Sebastian keeps his hand on me, and I try to look like it's completely natural that we would be touching. Like he touches me like this all the time.

For one pose, I place my hand on his chest and look up at him, smiling all the time. I'm sure the press, and the label, will eat that one up.

It takes far too long, but we eventually make it into the venue properly. I haven't been to many of these awards shows yet, so it's not normal for me at all. I can't help but gape at the lavish decor and place settings.

We're led to a table towards the back, which is fine with me. Sebastian plays the gentleman well, holding out my chair for me to sit. I could almost believe he was actually into me with this treatment. I certainly know better though.

We're seated in the human section of the auditorium, and it very quickly becomes obvious as to why that might be an issue. Sebastian's chair is far too small for him. It's almost comical, his giant body in the chiavari chair.

"Don't laugh." He warns.

But that just sets me off. If there's one thing about me, I cannot hold in a good giggle to save my life. Sebastian's mouth quirks slightly, and I know he's struggling to keep up with his gloomy guy demeanor.

I sober up as some other humans nervously join us at our table. I can tell that they are unhappy with the seating arrangement, they sneer and I can't help but curl in on myself a bit.

Sebastian scoots his chair closer to mine to give the woman next to him breathing room. She looks ready to pass out. I try to give her a gentle, reassuring smile. But the scowl she gives me hurts. I've done nothing to this woman. I kind of wish we had sat in the monster section at this rate.

The man next to me has arrived, and he seems polite enough, giving me a small smile. Sebastian grunts, scooching closer to me and putting his arm around the back of my chair. My body is pressed flush against him now. The woman next to him must have really been creeping him out.

The waiters avoid Sebastian like a plague, setting his drinks down and sprinting away as fast as they can.

"Do you have everything you need?" He asks, surprising me. The announcement has gone out that they are starting the show in five minutes.

"A back up drink would be nice."

He signals to a waiter and has a drink in front of me in seconds, along with a glass of water.

"Don't forget to stay hydrated."

Who is this man?! Sebastian is *doting* on me. I'd almost believe someone had done a body swap on him, if he hadn't been pressed up against me the entire time. I haven't been able to help myself either, leaning into his embrace a little.

I could almost believe this ruse myself, settling in to watch the show.

I've noticed that the other humans have been giving me disapproving looks all evening, but they haven't dared with Sebastian. It's pretty wild considering they're clearly annoyed with me because of him. They're all cowards, that's where their hatred stems from. It's kind of powerful for me to realize that.

The rest of the show goes on without a hitch. I can see a few shots of myself and Sebastian make it on to the cameras, so I'm careful to keep my happy mask in place.

I'm yawning by the time the show finishes up. The other people at our table scatter at the first chance they get, desperate to get away from us.

"How about we sit here for a sec while the crowd disperses." I suggest.

Sebastian nods, then his eyes shift to behind me. I notice that the man who sat next to me hasn't left yet, and he's staring at us.

I turn slightly, and he speaks to me.

"Are you two *really* together? I haven't been able to figure it out all night, why a pretty girl like you would be interested in *him*."

How dare he? I thought his smile was kind earlier, but now he just looks creepy. I place my hand over Sebastian's on the table.

"Yes, we're together. Not that it's any of your business. And for your information, he's a way better lay than any human guy I've ever been with.

"Let's go," I stand, holding out my hand for Sebastian's. We walk away before the man can respond.

Sebastian doesn't address the incident as we wade through the crowd to leave. I'm getting kind of used to his silence at this point, anyway.

I'm relieved when we finally make it back to our car, my feet throbbing. Sebastian holds open the door for me, so I slide inside.

Disappointment rolls over me as Sebastian sits as far away from me as he can again. It feels like we're back to square one. And you know what? I'm pissed. Matilda completely disappeared earlier as well.

I'm fuming, actually. I'm so mad at everyone right now. I definitely let myself feel the fantasy as if it was real tonight. It's no one's fault but mine.

Well, I'm done. If this is how Sebastian wants this to go, then fine. That's *exactly* how it will go.

Chapter 8

"The label has had some interesting feedback from the press." Frank states.

"Go on then," I encourage. I have been interrupted from my morning routine yet again. My vinyl certainly not playing, and my coffee going cold. My fuse with Frank has been getting shorter and shorter.

"Well, all of your dates so far have been to award shows and other red carpet events. There has been suspicion that your relationship is not even real."

The fact that he says it like it's a shock is absolutely hilarious.

"Well, it's *not* real. So what do they need us to do next?" Obviously there's a great big plan incoming.

"It's nothing crazy, Flora, relax. It's a change of scenery that they're looking for, that's all."

I run my hands through my hair, tugging on it.

"You're going to meet with him this afternoon. Go for a walk in the park together. Trust me, it will be much easier than the dates you've been doing so far."

"Fine." I hang up. I don't know how they expect me to be writing an album at the moment when I have to drop everything at their behest.

The easiest thing to do these days is just agree. I switch my phone to 'Do Not Disturb' and go back out on the balcony to finish my coffee in the sun.

Sebastian Orville and I have been on four dates now. Four. Each and every one of them has gone the same. He picks me up in the limo, we don't talk until we're at the event, and then he goes right back to ignoring me in the car again. I haven't lost my mind again the way I did the first time. I've been matching his energy, it's easier that way.

That's such a lie, it's getting harder each time. I've lost sight of why we're even doing this now too. No one seems to be getting the message we set out for. I don't get to see the media on the monster side, but the human side is pretty bad. I haven't had any in-person confrontations yet, surprisingly. But the media online is portraying me as a traitor to my kind. Or at least, that's what the big news channels are saying.

The smaller channels, the more art and music focused groups, have been so supportive. That has been lovely. People are coming out more and more to question why we are taught to hate like this.

I think of that side when I don't feel like doing this anymore.

There's also been talk from Fortune Records about setting up a studio that both humans and monsters will work from, right on the edge of town, where both sides meet. I don't know how much of that is true, but it does make me hopeful.

Who knows, maybe I'll meet a dragon shifter there that isn't a gloomy asshole.

Doubtful.

***

We follow our usual routine when the car comes to pick me up.

Silence.

I sigh, watching out the window to see where we are going. It looks like we're heading to Center Park, a place where no one really even goes. Half of it is in the Monster side of the city, the other in the human side.

I get out of the car before Sebastian gets up. I'm wearing a cute little leggings and tank set in bright yellow, covered up by a cozy pastel blue hoodie. My blue sneakers are what have me hopping out before him.

I'm always wearing some sort of stupid contraption on my feet when we normally have these dates, so it's nice to be able to hop out before him and set the pace.

I look back to make sure he's following. I haven't really looked at him yet, which was definitely a mistake. He's wearing gray sweatpants that hang low on his hips, paired with a black hoodie and sneakers. Ugh, why do men have to look so good in sweatpants.

"Race ya!" I call, setting off at a sprint, my ponytail swinging behind me. I need to get away from him before I lose it again.

He easily out-paces me, slipping by before I've even started really.

"How about we walk," he says, looking pained.

I slow my pace to a walk. "Sure," I say. He really does look in pain. Maybe he has an injury that he doesn't want to tell me about.

So we walk, hand in hand, while some very obvious paparazzi take photos of us. It's all so planned and staged, it's laughable that this is what's supposed to make us look more genuine.

We're barely walking for five minutes when we're told that we're all good to go. Frank was right, this kind of date was easier.

When we're settled back in the car, both our phones ding at the same time. I look down to see a text from Frank:

That went well. You'll be going out again tomorrow night to a club. Monster side of town. Pick up is at 11:30 pm.

Sebastian glares at his phone, his teeth grinding as he tosses it onto the seat next to him.

"Are you OK?" I ask him, gently.

He refuses to answer, refuses to even look at me.

Not for the first time, I wonder why Sebastian is even doing this whole PR stunt.

Chapter 9

I have no idea what to wear.

I'm in my second bedroom, turned closet and music room. Clothes are strewn everywhere, a pastel mess all over my floor.

Reclining in my desk chair, I groan at the sight before me. The car will be here to pick me up in an hour and I haven't done my eye makeup or my hair yet. Plus, I need to pack an overnight bag. We're staying in a hotel tonight after our date, for full authenticity. Frank has assured me that there are two separate rooms booked, at least.

Today, I also learned that the rumors about the studio are true. Fortune Records will be the first company to establish a work space where both humans and monsters will be working together. And who better to mark the grand opening than their power couple of choice. So that's later this week. God, I will have to pick an outfit for that too.

No, I have to focus on tonight. What do you even wear to a club filled with monsters? Everything I own is colorful, and I'm worried that I will stick out like a sore thumb. Am I stereotyping by assuming that they'll all be wearing dark clothes? Ugh, maybe.

When in doubt, be yourself, Flora. Yeah, I can do that. If I could wear anything tonight, what would it be? I pick out a dress that I haven't gotten to wear yet. It's tight through my waist, with a little ruffle that starts midway down my but. It has puffy off the shoulder cap sleeves too, and it's in a gorgeous pastel floral print.

I might regret wearing these if they get ruined, but I pull out my sage green over the knee suede boots. Yes, this is fun! It's giving more my onstage persona though, but why not go for it? Flora on stage is way more confident than Flora off stage.

I'll need to pick out a cute wig too, then. I run my fingers through my long pink, wavy one. Perfect. I will do some fun makeup and then put this on properly.

Let's see if Sebastian can ignore me in this.

***

All in all, I end up being ready a few minutes late, the car idling outside of my building when I get downstairs.

I'm super happy with the outfit I ended up choosing. I feel fun, and I will need to bring that energy for the both of us tonight, no doubt.

Sebastian is wearing black trousers and a gray button-up with the top few buttons undone. That glimpse of his chest has me nearly drooling a little, the indent between his pecs clearly visible.

He does a definite double take as I get into the car. My weekend bag is weighing me down and I stumble a little. He darts up and takes my bag from me, setting it on the floor.

"Thanks," I say, simply. I'm not expecting any kind of response, this is the best greeting I've had in a long time.

"You look different," he says, looking at my hair.

"Oh, this?" I twirl a strand around my finger. "I usually wear stuff like this on stage. It's part of my act. But you wouldn't know that, I guess..."

It's crazy how we've now spent all this time together and we still know essentially nothing about the other. I don't know anything about the type of music he makes.

We fall back into our usual silence. I notice him glancing at me more than usual though.

The car crosses the border into the monster side of town. I've never been here before, so I can't help but look out the window. Everything looks similar enough for now, but we're definitely in the downtown area.

"Did someone prep you for this?" Sebastian's deep timbre reaches me from the other side of the car.

I shrug, "The update that I got earlier was that there would be paparazzi there to photograph us at the entrance. But that we were going to have to rely on candid shots from the public from inside to get out there."

"No, Flora," he looks at me with disapproval. "Were you prepped on how to behave at the club, or what to expect?"

I am stunned into silence, I think that's the longest sentence I've ever heard him utter. I shake my head slowly.

"You're going to be surrounded by monsters tonight. You're going into the lion's den."

Well, I mean, I was nervous about going to a club full of monsters. But I also have maybe underestimated it, judging by his demeanor. Like, it must be important if he's been talking to me this much.

"So all monsters aren't the silent, grumpy type?" I tease.

"Can you be serious for one second, Flora?" He snaps at me, his voice edged sharp like a knife.

My lip wobbles and I blink back tears. His words sting and I feel like a scolded school child. I only try to be fun to bring up his mood a bit. Besides, I don't believe for a second that he'd actually let something happen to me. I look away, curling in on myself a little, and trying to ignore him. I'm so done with his shit right now.

A warmth appears at my side a moment later, a hand gently touching my arm.

"Hey, I'm sorry."

"Too bad," I sniffle, pushing him away. He lets go of me, but he stays close.

"Listen, I didn't mean to snap at you. It's just..." I turn to look at him as his mind wanders. He runs a hand through his stupid, perfect hair. I envy him that, wondering what it feels like.

"It could be dangerous, Flora." I watch his mouth as he speaks, his plush lips barely move as he practically whispers. "Stay close to me. I'll look after you."

I glance up to his eyes and get lost in them for a moment. But then, of course, he pulls away. He moves back to his original seat.

What is wrong with me? Why do I keep letting my guard down around him? I tip my head back and stare at the roof of the car until it pulls to a stop.

I know we're here by the sounds outside. Sebastian moves to get up.

"Please, don't." I tell him. "Give me a second, for once."

"Well, forgive me for wanting to get this over with." He quips back.

Great. I guess we're in the 'snide remarks' phase of our relationship. I love this for me. Truly. Maybe going back to silence wouldn't be so bad, after all.

I close my eyes and ask for the universe to give me some fucking strength.

I don't give him a warning, opening the door and stepping out.

Oh God, this is a lot. All manner of creatures are crowded around the entrance to the club. There's a few groups smoking to the left, a line waiting for entrance to the right. There are a couple paparazzi at the door as well, already taking photos of us.

There is also not one single human in sight. It's not that I expected there to be, but it's still jarring to experience. There are so many different types of monsters around me, that I can't really take in any details. It's a sea of horns, pointed ears, wings, different colored skins, and tails.

A body presses up flush against my back, the familiar feeling of Sebastian's warmth. He bends over and I look up to see what he's doing. He looms closer, a predatory look in his gaze. He's not going to kiss me, is he? Fuck, I can't turn away if he does, there's photos being taken.

He bypasses my lips, his nose nuzzling my neck softly. I feel the shift in the air as he breathes in deeply. A rush of tingles flush through me from head to toe, a swarm of butterflies battling in my stomach.

The man is sniffing me... why am I so into it? He takes his time over it, too. My eyes flutter closed, but I can feel many gazes burn into me.

I'm out of place here. I'm not wanted. These people have been taught to hate me.

All this time, I've been thinking about how I'm going to help the humans with their hatred for monsters. I haven't really thought about it the other way around. Am I enough to make that kind of change on this side of the fence?

Sebastian slowly pulls away from me, and I feel the absence of him deep in my gut. He takes my hand, closing the car door behind us with a slam. I startle a little at the noise, and he gives my hand a comforting squeeze. He tugs me along with him to the entrance, keeping me close.

The doorman nods to Sebastian, who holds out our hands to him. Before I can freak out at the gesture, the massive green skinned man places a black ink stamp on our wrists. Oh, I giggle a little in relief, it's only an entry stamp. It's a club, Flora, relax.

The doorman, who has *tusks*, gestures to Sebastian where our private area is located, up on the balcony. He leads me forward again. In true club fashion, you still have to walk through a packed crowd, no matter who you are. Except no one touches me at all. They actively push at one another to avoid touching me.

The music here is kind of different too, a much heavier beat than I'm used to. I can almost feel it in my bones.

We get about half way, or at least I think so, when a willowy beauty with a stunning flowing mini dress approaches us. Or, approaches Sebastian, I guess. She runs her fingers lightly down Sebastian's arm, a gleam in her eyes. Irrationally, I am filled with rage watching her touch him.

"I know that I can promise you a much better night than this... lousy *human*."

Well, fuck her. Before I can respond or come to my own defense, Sebastian growls at her, his eyes glowing bright. Did I think he was growling before, when I heard that rumble from his chest? I was wrong. This was loud, and I can hear the menace behind it.

He pushes past her, switching which hand of mine he's holding. The hand that had been holding mine grips me tight around the waist. I'm enveloped by him as he stomps the last bit of the walk to our booth. The other monsters physically cringe away from his anger. I kind of feel protected, though?

I feel a little manhandled as he guides me to our booth and sits me down in a seat. He slides in next to me and puts an arm around me, pulling me tight against him. I'm into it, having him handle me like that, placing me where I need to be. I lightly place a hand on his thigh, trying to look cozy. I'm hyper aware that the other people here could be taking photos of us at any time.

"What do you want to drink?" He asks me.

"Umm... do you think they would have a whiskey and coke?" He looks down at me, a bewildered look on his face.

"You *do* know that we have the same food and drink here?" He asks, incredulously.

"Maybe...?"

He rolls his eyes at me, a slight grin tugging at his mouth. Sebastian signals to the waiter, a devil looking man with red skin and horns. He orders our drinks, asking for them to bring the unopened bottles to open in front of us.

"Why did you ask for it like that?" I ask, once the waiter has left, his pointed tail swinging behind him.

"I'm being careful," is all he says.

OK, cool. So I'm in a club filled with monsters, and my drinks need to be opened in front of me in case I get spiked. Fun.

I'm back to receiving the silent treatment again, I realize. The waiter brings us our drinks, making a big performance of opening them. I would laugh if Sebastian wasn't staring at the poor man with lethal poise, watching intently. He takes a sip of his drink, sitting casually, and not saying a single fucking word.

God, this man drives me insane.

"Can't we just get along, please?" I trace a drip of condensation on my glass with my finger, leaving a clean line behind. "I know that you're disgusted by me, but this would be easier if we could get along. I know you don't talk much, but—"

"You don't disgust me, Flora." He cuts across me. "Quite the opposite, really. I'm disgusted by myself."

What?! I can't even begin to decipher that. I open my mouth to speak, but he downs his drink and stands abruptly. He holds out a hand to me.

"We're going to dance now." Sebastian's voice holds no room for argument.

Chapter 10

Sebastian doesn't give me time to ponder his abrupt decision to dance. I'm half-dragged with him to the floor.

The bodies here don't move away as much, all too drunk or lost in the music to notice. I wish I had gotten to drink more. Luckily, I'm always up for a good dance.

I am surprised by how smoothly Sebastian moves to the music. Well, at least until I remember that he's also a musician. He's bound to have some level of rhythm.

The deep, pulsing beat of the music flows through my veins and I lose myself in it. Sebastian doesn't touch me as much now, only a gentle graze here and there. It's almost more a tease than the manhandling from earlier.

Closing my eyes, I let the sound wash over me, twisting my body to the bass.

I barely drank half of my drink, but I'm already feeling buzzed. I stumble a little and my eyes open as I catch myself. I look around, but I don't see Sebastian anymore. I must have lost him in the crowd.

Surprisingly, I don't really seem to mind all that much. I continue dancing, ending up in the middle of a group of creatures. Now this is who I pictured coming to the monster club. Pale skin, dark eyes and hair, and a goth aesthetic.

I giggle at them, wanting to tell them about it, but I can't seem to speak. It doesn't bother me all that much though, I just want to dance.

The group that I'm dancing with are fun, they have such a nice calming energy that I want to sink into. One woman moves towards me and is dancing with only me now. Every so often, her hand grazes my arm and she looks at me with her black eyes.

Someone else is dancing behind me, and I feel them move in and grip my waist. At first, I don't like the feeling, but the woman looks me in the eyes again and I forget that it bothered me.

The person behind me starts to pull me back against them and I don't like it. I shut my eyes, trying to figure out what is happening. They grope at me, grabbing my boob hard. I scream out.

"You were supposed to keep her entranced." An annoyed voice says as the person behind me pulls my head back roughly, baring my throat.

"Stop! Get off me!" I scream, trying to pull away. Their grip is like stone though and there is nothing I can do to stop them.

I catch a glimpse of another one of the group launching themselves at me. I want to shut my eyes, but I can only stare as I see my death coming for me.

Hands grip at the shoulders of my attacker, picking him up and tossing him out of the way. My captor releases me, fleeing quickly, as Sebastian looms over me.

Sebastian holds out a hand to me and I fling myself at him. He pulls me close, holding me delicately.

I turn to see the woman with the eyes, but look away quickly. I think she had me in some sort of trance.

"Do not come near," Sebastian's voice is low but carries over the pulsing music. "One step closer, one more attempt to hurt her, and I will *end* you."

I bury my head in Sebastian's chest. The woman must have gotten the picture, because he holds me away slightly to look at me. He swipes his thumb along my cheek. Oh, I think I'm crying. Everything feels numb right now.

He lifts me as if I weigh nothing, turning to leave. A vicious growl rumbles in his chest, his body flashing hot for a moment. I tense as wings sprout from his back, along with the sound of tearing fabric.

Sebastian launches us into the air and flies us back to our seats up on the balcony. I know I'm in shock, because my reaction to the wings is not nearly what it should be. They're gone quickly once we land, his shirt a torn up mess that barely clings to him.

He barely notices himself though, settling me down on a seat and bending down in front of me. He pushes my hair back from my face, holding me softly. Keeping his hands there, he turns to a waiter and demands they bring water and napkins.

"I-I'm sorry," I mumble, looking down at the floor. "Y-You t-told me to st-stay with you."

"Shh..." He strokes away a rolling tear with his thumb. "You didn't do anything wrong, sunshine."

I look up at him, my reality sinking in a little and I realize that I'm trembling.

"Come here," he pulls me against his chest. He strokes my back, and I sob into him. I know I should be embarrassed but I can't bring myself to feel it right now. All I am seeking is comfort.

"Drink a little water for me." There is a low command in Sebastian's voice that I don't question. I lean back and take the bottle that he offers. I sip at it a little while he grabs the napkins and dabs at my cheeks.

"Can I check you over?" He asks me. I nod, still sipping.

Sebastian runs his hands over my neck, lifting my wig gently to look closer. Then he checks both my wrists.

"OK, let's get you out of here." He takes my water bottle from me, setting it on the table. Sebastian wraps his arm around my shoulders, the other under my knees, as he lifts me up bridal style.

People keep their distance as we leave, but I hate their gazes on me. I burrow my head into Sebastian's neck and breathe in his calming scent.

The fresh air is cool when we get outside. Sebastian must have already called the car because we get inside quickly and efficiently. He sits down and keeps me on his lap.

"Do you want me to take you home?"

I lift my head, sniffling. "No, we said we would go to the hotel."

"That was before..." he shifts so that he can look at me properly. "Say the word, and I will take you home. Consequences be damned."

I shake my head, loosening my grip. I didn't realize that I had been grabbing his shirt so tightly. I pull away altogether, shifting to sit on the seat next to him.

"No. I'll be OK. I was just in shock." He still has an arm around my shoulders and I use it to anchor myself. "Besides, I'd prefer not to be alone right now."

"Even if you're stuck with a silent, grumpy type?" He grins slightly, using my words from earlier to tease me. I push him away, giggling.

"I need to change this," he gestures to his torso.

Oh, yes he does, his shirt is torn from his wings and damp from my tears. Sebastian pulls away from me, moving to the back of the car to root through his bag. He pulls out a simple white t-shirt.

I don't even pretend to look away as he tugs his shirt over his head. His back ripples with muscles and I want to reach out and feel them. The white t-shirt he pulls on is tight around his biceps, the white contrasting against his dark skin.

Sebastian moves back to sit next to me, but he keeps his hands to himself this time.

"We should be there pretty soon, it's not far."

Chapter 11

"What do you mean, there's only one room booked?" Sebastian's voice is lined with deadly intent.

Unfortunately, the man behind the reception desk doesn't look phased at all. He's huge, even bigger than Sebastian, with green skin and tusks coming from his mouth.

I had used my phone's camera in the car to make myself look presentable before we went into the hotel. But I'm close to crying again, now. The receptionist has told us that there is only one room booked in the hotel for both of us.

It's too late at night to be calling Frank for a fix, and honestly I just want to close myself off from the world and relax for a bit.

"Can't we book another room?" I ask, quietly. "I don't mind paying for it..."

"There aren't any. We're fully booked." The receptionist's gruff voice replies.

I tug on Sebastian's elbow, trying to get his attention.

"It's OK. I don't mind sharing, and I think I would like the company tonight." I lean up slightly to whisper, "I'm a little scared to be on my own here, if I'm being honest."

Is Sebastian kind of a dick at the best of times? Yes. But do I feel safe with him? Yes. Does that make me certifiably insane? Also yes.

"If you're sure..."

I nod. Sebastian holds out his hand for the key card. The receptionist places it in his hand and instructs us on how to get to our room.

We make our way to the elevator, Sebastian carrying both our bags in one hand like they weigh nothing. I follow him into it and watch as he presses the button to our floor.

"What?" he asks me, a slight grin on his face. "I can see you thinking. You want to ask me something."

I blush, it's not fair that he can tell that.

"Well... it's only... what kind of monster was that man? The receptionist, I mean."

Sebastian chuckles, showing his teeth a little and I squirm at the sight. He's much more relaxed now, and it's really nice to see.

"He was what we call an orc. We also aren't called *men*," he chuckles a little again, almost to himself more than for me. "That's a human term. We're referred to as males and females. Or whatever you want that's in between, of course. But we're certainly *not* men and women."

The elevator doors open and he steps out into the hall-way first. I quickly follow behind him, a little afraid of being on my own here.

Our room is simple, a giant bed and a small table with two chairs. There's a small bathroom through a door, and that's it really. I've definitely stayed in nicer places, but it's fine. I wanted to get away from the world for a bit. Going home would not have been the distraction that I needed.

"This reeks of Karl..." Sebastian mutters under his breath.

"What?" I ask him. Wasn't Karl his manager?

"Nothing, my manager likes to play *pranks* on me some-times." He sets our bags on the floor next to the bed. "I can sleep on the floor."

I burst into laughter, patting him playfully on the chest. "Hilarious! As if you would fit on this floor. It's fine, we'll both sleep on the bed. It's huge, there's plenty of room for us both, and we're both adults. We can control ourselves."

I laugh a little more to myself as I bend down and root through my bag to get my cosmetics bag and pajamas.

"I'm going to go change out of this dress," I gesture down at my uncomfortable ensemble. "Do they have room service here? I'm starving. Maybe you could order us food?"

He grunts, which I take as a yes, and lock myself into the bathroom.

God, I look rough. I rest my hands on the counter as I lean forward, examining myself in the mirror. I didn't do as great of a job as I had thought with tidying myself up in the car. There are still tear streaks in my makeup. Although, I do have to say that my wig stayed pretty much in place.

I spray my wig glue remover onto my hairline before taking off my boots and dress. Surprisingly, my boots didn't get a single mark on them, which is impressive. My wig comes off easily, I've really honed my technique at this point. I scoop up my natural hair into a messy bun and wash off my makeup.

I wasn't expecting to have company when I chose my pajamas for tonight. My high waisted blue shorts and baby tee not leaving much to the imagination. A little strip of my stomach shows, and I know my ass cheeks are hanging out. I really can't bring myself to care, though. Sebastian isn't into me, anyway.

Or is he, though? In the heat of everything that happened, I had forgotten what he said to me before we danced. Sebastian had told me that he wasn't disgusted with me. But that didn't necessarily mean he was into me, either.

Surely, his behavior so far in our weird relationship would have been much better if he was interested. I sigh, applying my skincare and putting all my things away.

Sebastian is still wearing the same white t-shirt when I come back into the room. He's switched out his jeans for gray sweatpants, the waist folded over once to show a sexy strip of his dark skin. I can see the beginning of his 'v' shaped muscles pointing south, there are some scales there too.

He's watching me, his jaw clenched tight.

"I didn't know what you wanted," he runs a hand through his luscious hair. "But I ordered us food. I got some different things. I'll eat what you don't like."

I go to reply, but then he reaches up, pulling his hair back into a bun at the back of his head. His stretch shows off more of his impressive abdomen. Holy hell, the man is hot. I mean, the *male* is hot. So damn hot.

I look away, packing my things in my bag and putting my wig away properly. I hear the bathroom door shut, Sebastian having gone in there.

I sigh, placing my hands on my hips and looking around the room. At least the bed is big, I guess Monster beds would need to be a lot bigger than human ones. I plop onto it, sitting cross-legged and picking up my phone to scroll.

I ignore all my notifications and text Rosie:

Don't panic if you see a video online with me looking disheveled. It was a misunderstanding and I'm totally fine and safe.

On second thought, I text that to my parents too.

I'm a little chilly, actually. I look around the room and spot Sebastian's hoodie. I'm sure he won't mind me borrowing it for a bit. He runs ridiculously hot anyway, he'll be fine.

There's a knock at the door, which must be the food. I hop up, toss my phone on the bed and open the door.

A beautiful person with blue skin is on the other side, a cart filled with different covered dishes in front of them.

They do a double take when they see me. They probably didn't know that there would be a human answering, so I don't blame them.

"Thank you." I say, moving to take the cart from them.

"I will bring it in, Madame." I go to move aside to let him past when Sebastian looms behind me. He places a hand on my waist to hold me in place, the other on the door frame as he leans forward.

"*We'll* take it in." He is cordial, but I can hear the menace in his voice.

"Of course, Sir." The monster nods nervously, backing away down the hallway.

Sebastian waits until they are out of sight before moving me aside to bring in the cart. Once the door is shut, he turns on me, hands on his hips.

"You are far too trusting, Flora." He tuts at me, stepping forward. I move away, my back hitting the wall, essentially trapping myself in. "Do not let anyone else in the room. Do not wander from me. I can't protect you if you keep doing silly, trusting things."

There's a desperate sound in his voice, and I realize that he might also be a bit shaken from the events of the night.

"You're right. I think I keep forgetting where we are." I place a hand on his chest and look up at him. "I'll behave. If we're in the monster side of town for a date again, I mean."

The heat of his chest warms my hand, reminding me that I was a little chilly. I shiver a little, "I borrowed your hoodie, I hope you don't mind. I was cold."

"You're cold because you're still in shock." He pulls away from me. "You need to eat."

Sebastian sets up the food cart next to the table, sitting down and gesturing for me to do the same. He pours me a glass of water, and only then do I actually realize how *much* food there is.

"It's on the company account, and they owe us." He says, reading my expression perfectly. He goes through the long list of what he ordered and asks me to pick what I want.

I end up choosing a bacon cheeseburger, tater tots, and I grab a few onion rings too for good measure.

Sebastian was right. I did need the food.

I start to perk up as I eat, chatting away enough for the both of us.

"Oh, I meant to ask you something," he looks up from his sandwich, ready for my question. "What did you do when we arrived at the club? It felt like you were smelling me? I don't know, the cameras were going and I didn't want to look weirded out."

A deep flush colors his cheeks and he coughs, choking a little on his food.

"I'm not sure you really want to know, Flora."

I shrug, tossing a tater tot into my mouth, the greasy salty flavor popping on my tongue. "Try me."

Does he think he can scare me out of hearing the answer? He clearly doesn't know one thing about me. I'm like a dog with a bone when it comes to a piece of gossip.

He sighs, setting his food down and wiping his hands on a napkin.

"OK, I'll tell you. But before you get mad, I thought it was the best thing to do for your safety. Well, clearly it wasn't enough of a deterrent, but I thought it was going to be."

He pauses for a moment, so I set my own food down. Something tells me I am about to hate what he is going to say, with the way he set that up.

"Go on..." I encourage.

"I was sort of... it was me marking you as mine, in a way. It's a way of us monsters saying that we're claiming a mate. But I did it because I wanted to make sure that they knew you were off limits. That you were spoken for... by me..."

Oh. Why did that not make me angry? I think back through the moment again, about how good it had felt. I *liked* it. And now, knowing what it was... my pussy throbs. A claiming... that sounded amazing, for some weird reason.

Don't get me wrong, I am into some kinky shit, anyway. But this hits somewhere new for me, unlocking something new.

I shrug my shoulders, "I think it worked for the most part."

He relaxes a little, his shoulders dropping slightly. We both get back to eating and speaking about nothing in particular.

We chill in our seats and continue chatting once we're done eating. I ask him about his music, and he plays a little for me.

I'm not sure what I expected, but it wasn't this. His music certainly has traditional folk roots underlying everything, but there was a bluesy and rock influence there too. There were also layers of sound added post-production, which he admitted that his producer was behind. It created a whole new sound that I hadn't heard anything like before.

I cringe a little when he asks to hear mine. It's not nearly as good as his, and he's been on the scene a lot longer than me too. His music has a refined sound that I haven't achieved yet.

"Please? I showed you mine." He teases, playfully pouting at me. That is a totally unfair tactic on his part.

"Fine, but please remember, I haven't released my first album yet. Just an EP and a few singles." I play my favorite piece for him. My sound is a lot more techno heavy than his. It's not that I make club music, but I want every song I create to have an energy about it, for it to give the listener *life*.

I pointedly stare at the phone as the song plays, refusing to see his reaction. Silence fills the room as the song finishes. His slow clap has me looking up.

Sebastian has a huge grin on his face, which isn't something I've seen before. He's beautiful when he smiles.

"That was amazing, Flora." He leans forward, an excited energy about him. "And you've really only produced the EP and a few other tracks?"

I nod, a slow smile radiating from me. I preen with his praise.

"Can you play me more?"

***

At some point, we move to the bed. We continue playing music for each other. Not only our own, but selections from our favorite artists, too.

It's so cool being able to hear music from monsters, and I think Sebastian feels the same way about the human music.

We talk and talk about music for hours, learning so much from one another. I actually can't believe how much he is speaking with me. I think that maybe small talk isn't his strong suit. But when you get Sebastian Orville talking about music... that's when you really get to hear his voice.

It must be after 3 am when my eyes start to droop shut, my voice slowing.

"Time for sleep." Sebastian tells me. I nod my head and let him pull the covers up over me.

I sort of sense him snuggling in on the other side of the bed, but I fall asleep too quickly to know for sure.

***

I feel like I am on a heated mattress. A firm, *heated* mattress.

It feels good, so I snuggle in further, sighing happily to myself. I do love cozy mornings.

It takes me a moment to understand that I don't wrap my legs around mattresses, and that mattresses don't hold me back.

Sebastian.

Holy shit. I am currently draped over Sebastian's chest, my leg wrapped around his waist, my hand fisted in his t-shirt. God, he feels good.

It's been a long time since I've been draped over a man like this. Never has it been with one so big, meaning I fit snugly on his torso. His arms are wrapped around me, and I feel cocooned in the best way possible.

I decide to stay here for a bit. His steady breathing tells me he is still asleep, and I want to enjoy the feeling of the moment. I know it's never going to happen again.

After a while, I realize that I should get up before he wakes. Maybe I can get out of the bed without him noticing. That way he won't be embarrassed by what happened.

I carefully extract myself from his grip. Apart from one hitch in his breath, I don't think I wake him. I slide out of the bed, grabbing my bag and heading into the bathroom to get changed.

When I come back into the room, he is still fast asleep. So I fold his hoodie and put it on top of his bag.

"Sebastian," I whisper, trying to wake him gently. No response. Nada.

I end up having to call his name quite loudly to wake him up. He is super groggy, and extremely adorable. With his messy hair and rumpled clothes, he looks *normal*.

I sit down and scroll through my phone while he slowly potters about, getting ready for the day.

***

I'm home within the hour, questioning if any of it was real. Neither of us spoke much in the car, but we were both exhausted from the late night and lack of coffee.

Chapter 12

I restlessly roll over in my bed. I hardly slept a wink, but the sun shining through my window tells me that morning has come, yet again.

It's been a week since my sleepover with Sebastian, and no one has been in touch to schedule another date for us. We never exchanged phone numbers either, so it's not like I could text him. But also, we're not exactly on texting status anyway. I don't even know *what* we are.

I turn over, pulling the cover over my head to block out the sun. I wish I could hide from myself that easily. All of my thoughts have been trailing back to Sebastian lately. I am replaying different moments in my mind, but the one

I keep coming back to was how it felt to be wrapped up in his arms in bed.

Oh God, I'm so fucked.

I'm going to see him today, too. Against all odds, Fortune Records has set up their new studios in a week. Which makes me think that they've had all this in the works a lot longer than that. Today, we're having a grand opening, along with a little showcase of our artists.

Which means I'm going to have to perform in front of Sebastian. I gulp as I think about it. I'm not normally one for stage fright, but this is terrifying. To top it all off, we're to play 'get to know each other' games to break the ice with our new colleagues.

I am excited about the studio though. I'm supposed to be writing my album at the moment, and I think it will be a fun change of pace to work there. Besides, I'm curious to see the monsters in a normal work setting. I imagine it's kind of like when you see a teacher outside of school, doing something completely normal.

I've been working on the early stages of my new music recently, so it will be good to get back into the studio with Alex again. Alex is amazing, they have produced all of my work until now and I wouldn't be able to create my sound without their collaboration. They'll be there today too.

So will Daisy and Cleo. I'm doing a full out performance, so I have to have my dancers. I'm actually going to pick them up on the way there.

I'm trying to shift my thoughts to be more positive. It's almost working, until I remember that I'm going to see Sebastian and his band play today. Or at least I assume I am. I haven't actually considered if every artist under the label will be playing. I hope he does, I've been listening to his music on repeat all week.

The label released a new music app to feature both human and monster artists. I've been listening to so much cool new music, and it's been inspiring for me. Sebastian's music, especially. I've been sharing some of it with Alex, and even they can't figure out how some of the technical layering works. So they're excited to try and meet Sebastian's producer today.

I sigh, rolling out of bed. It's time to get ready and get to work.

I pull up into my space in the lot, then double check that my parking card matches the number.

"This is a *good* spot." Cleo calls from the back seat.

It is a good spot, too good a spot. Since when do I get to park this close to the building?

I switch off the ignition and turn to look at Daisy and Cleo.

"Are you guys as nervous as I am?"

Daisy nods as Cleo declares, "I'm excited! I want a monster boyfriend like you, Flora." She sticks out her tongue at me, teasing.

I look away quickly, starting to pack up my purse properly and then checking my hair in the rear view mirror. I hate lying to my friends about Sebastian, but I would hate breaking that airtight NDA even more.

Lucky for me, apparently we're very convincing at being together. Even my friends don't really see through it. Well, that's a lie. Rosie can tell that something's up, but she also knows that I would tell her if I could. So she doesn't ask.

"Come on, let's go in, already!" Cleo whines. I make eye contact with Daisy in the mirror and we share a look. Cleo was going to be a lot to handle today.

"Hang on a sec." I say. "Alex said that they'd be here in a few minutes. Let's wait for them and we can all go in together."

I take the time to look at the building. It's huge, looking more like a corporate office building from the outside. I guess they didn't need to worry about space in this part of town. It's located right on the border between the monsters and humans.

There's a monster making his way down the sidewalk right now, heading towards the building. He is dressed in a suit, well, his top half is. Instead of having legs, the rest of him is a giant snake. He carries a briefcase, so I assume that he's an important executive for the label.

"Still sure you want to get with a monster, Cleo?" I tease, seeing her jaw drop as she also notices him.

We're staring at him so intently, that we all jump when someone knocks on the passenger side window. I unlock the doors when I see it's Alex and they come and sit with us.

"Hey, love," I lean over to hug them in greeting.

"Hey girlies," Alex replies. "I'm incredibly nervous right now."

"Us too," Daisy quips.

I've done this before. I've met quite a few monsters now, and I know I can handle this.

"OK. Let's rip off this band aid." I open my door and walk around to the trunk, popping it open. The girls join me and we all grab our dance bags. We're already dressed for the performance today. I'm wearing my teal blue wig that's tied up into a pair of high bubble braids. I've paired it with white combat boots so I'm comfortable for the day. My outfit itself is a lavender baby tee and a teal mini skirt. I wanted to represent my onstage persona, but also go a little more casual for comfort more than anything else.

Not that this wig is comfortable at all. Sometimes I regret the wigs, but then I see the photos and video clips from performances and I'm so happy with them. I tasked Daisy and Cleo to wear their teal baby tees and lavender cargo pants, slung low on their hips. They can pull that look off so much better than me, my pants would literally fall down if I tried to wear them that low.

We make our way to the building and step inside. Cleo is first through the door, always the eager one. A female with snakes for hair meets us on the other side, a clipboard in hand.

"Hello to you all," she says. She checks us in and has us get in line to have new ID cards created.

***

I'm sitting across from a young orc female, Tabitha. She's pretty nice, and we've been chatting about wigs for the past ten minutes. She is fascinated by mine and wants to try out something new. I don't blame her since she told me that her black hair can't be bleached or colored.

The bell dings, and I promise to bring in a few products for her to try tomorrow.

We've been sort of playing a speed dating game, except it's for us to meet our new colleagues. I move to my next table, a female with dark purple hair sits across from me. We shake hands and a little spark zaps me.

"Oh, shit. Sorry!" She exclaims. "I normally have a bit more control over that, I promise. God, this is so embarrassing."

I laugh, trying to lighten the mood. "No, don't worry! It woke me up a little, that's all. I'm Flora, it's nice to meet you."

"Flora?" She looks at me closer, "Shit, I was expecting you to be blond. Sebastian's going to kill me. Oh God, please don't tell him I zapped you, he'll have my head!"

"Woah, it's OK! I promise, your secret is safe with me." I study her a little, wondering who she might be to Sebastian. She's beautiful, purple eyes to match her purple hair, with the palest skin. I try not to be jealous.

"Umm... so... what's your name?" I ask her.

"Oh! I'm Addison."

"Sebastian's producer?" she nods. "Oh, I am obsessed with you. Actually my own producer might be more so. Their name is Alex."

I point to a couple heads behind me, "you'll meet them soon. We've been trying to figure out some of the things that you've been doing on Sebastian's tracks and we literally can't. I would love if you sat down with us both some time. I'm working on a new album at the moment, so it would be so cool. Sorry, I'm totally commandeering the conversation!"

She grins at me slowly, a mischievous look on her face. "Firstly, thank you, I would love to sit down with you guys. Secondly," she leans forward, lowering her voice, "you are so different than I thought you would be. In a good way, don't get me wrong. I actually can't wait to see you and Sebastian together."

She glances to her right, and I realize that Sebastian is next in the line for me to talk to. I look away before he catches me staring. That means he's chatting to Cleo right now. Oh, I hope she is keeping it cool.

I shift my focus back to Addison, "Why? Because he's so chatty?"

Addison bursts out laughing at my sarcastic remark.

"Oh, I am glad that Sebastian finally has someone to keep him on his toes. He was getting far too comfortable."

I try to keep a happy mask on my face, but this is difficult. "I'm so sorry, Addison, but I need to excuse myself. I know we're going to chat lots soon anyway."

With that, I leave the table and head to the restroom. It's quiet, with everyone participating in the icebreakers. I turn on a tap and shove my wrists under, I feel far too hot all of a sudden. My chest heaves and I try to take in a slow, deep breath.

I look in the mirror and I feel like I don't recognize myself. I'm not a liar, it's not something that I've ever liked to do. And yet here I am, meeting a whole new group of people and trying to form connections. They're based on lies, it's all just one big lie and I can't stand it.

I only need to stay here until my turn with Sebastian would be over, and then I'll go back in. I hear the ding. Perfect, my time with Addison would be up now anyway. I'll wait until the next ding and I will go back in and pick up with the next person.

Yeah, that'll be fine. I lean against the counter, taking another deep breath.

The door to the restroom opens, and I grab a paper towel, pretending that I was finishing washing my hands.

In the mirror, I can see that it's Sebastian. He moves forward, looming over me. I want to lean back, I really do. I want to press myself against him and let him hold me.

"Are you OK?" He asks, he toys with the end of one of my braids.

"No, I'm not OK." I sigh, pulling my braid out of his hand and stepping away from him. "I hate that we're lying to everyone, to my friends. I've met so many people today and had to lie to their face and I'm sick of it."

"Flora, I know. I don't like doing it either. But we signed that—" The bell dings again, cutting across him.

"We should head back." I slip past him and move back into the room again.

***

I'm panting heavily, sweat dripping down my back. The wash of adrenaline flows through me and I relax a little. This is exactly what I needed.

Daisy, Cleo, and I just finished our set, and the staff of Fortune Records loved it. Or at least they applauded really loudly, with hoots and hollers for the girls. Who seemed to have made a few new friends with our icebreaker games earlier.

I laugh with them now, going to grab a drink of water. We move back out into the audience to watch whoever is next. I rest my head on Alex's shoulder as we join them in the seats.

"Eww, you're so sweaty, Flora!" They exclaim, but I giggle, switching to Cleo's shoulder instead. She wraps her arm around me and we enjoy the next few artist's performances.

When it's announced that Sebastian's next, I sit up a little straighter. I had gotten so wrapped up in my own performance, that I had forgotten all about his.

His band takes the stage. A tentacled male comes out first, drumsticks in his two hands, as well as in four of his tentacles. *That* was going to sound so cool. A giant minotaur, I learned what the bull-like creature was earlier, comes out next holding a bass guitar.

The crowd goes wild as Sebastian comes out, his guitar in hand. His hair hangs loose around his face, he wears faded and torn jeans with a vintage band t-shirt. He looks every bit the rock star. He also has his wings out.

I didn't look at them in too much detail last week, but they have a fascinating membranous quality, the black reflecting green under the lights.

I have to cross my legs, squirming in my seat a little bit. He looks far too attractive up there like that. All of my pent up horniness from the past week is letting itself be known. Then he smiles at the crowd with a cheeky grin. His eyes are searching the audience, until they find mine. He winks at me, before turning and strumming the first few bars of the song.

Holy shit, that did things to me. My pussy is throbbing with need. This is not good. I remind myself that it's all just for show, it's not real.

Daisy squeals, slapping me on the arm. "He winked at you!"

Daisy and Cleo both rock out a little too vigorously, but I can't help but laugh and join them as Sebastian plays and sings his song. His voice is somehow even better live than in his recordings. I am in awe of him.

Chapter 13

Alex and Hyacinth are fiddling around with some-thing on the sound mixing desk, so I sit and ob-serve.

Hyacinth is a new hire to our team, the label deciding that they could get us an extra pair of hands in the studio. She's essentially a trainee tech at the moment, but she's pretty good at what she does. She smiles sweetly at Alex, her chestnut eyes lighting up as she learns something new. She has an adorable innocence, and I think Alex wants to dote on her a little.

They finish up what they're doing and ask me to head back into the sound booth. I lay down a few different recordings of ad libs for a track we have been working on all day. I think it's starting to come together now, though. Especially once Alex does some post-production magic on it. I'm excited to see what they've learned from Addison too. They met up earlier in the week, bringing along the ever eager Hyacinth.

Once they're happy with the takes, I send Alex and Hyacinth off early. That way I can use the last bit of studio time we had booked to work on a piece I'm writing. To be honest, I'm struggling with the pressure a bit these days. Clearly, the label is putting more time and money into me. With the super close parking space, and the new sound tech. It's nice and all, but the more that they invest in me, the more pressure that I feel to perform at my best.

All that to say, I've been working a lot harder lately. Since the studio opened a week ago, I've been in here every day, working on my album and trying to make it perfect.

I sit down at the beautiful piano now and gently run through a few scales to warm up. Clipping my notebook to the stand, I read through the lyrics I already have. I start to test out different chord progressions, singing against them and trying to find a general tonality for the song. Once I'm happy with the key signature, I really get to work.

After a bit of time has passed, I'm pretty deep into the song, but there's one part that I can't seem to get right.

"Stop trying to resolve it," I jump at the sound of Sebastian's deep voice over the intercom. "Try a G minor instead."

I look behind me to the producer's seat, and sure enough, there he is. He looks so much larger behind the mixing desk than tiny Alex does.

"Stop looking at me and just try it."

I sigh, who let him in here? I do try what he says though, because it's a good idea. I play it once without singing and the effect is beautiful. Then I try it again, singing my line over it.

"Perfect." He says over the intercom again. "That line is really pretty, Flora.

"Can I come in?" He asks.

I nod and watch as he makes his way to the door of the booth. He comes in and pulls up a chair. Leaning forward, his forearms resting on his legs, he looks at me and speaks.

"You've run over into my studio time. But lucky for you, Addison isn't able to make it today. So I won't be doing any recording. I can stay and help you, if you like. Or I can fuck off and leave you to it."

I think it over. While I want him to leave me be, I do need his help. He did something great there and I want this song to be perfect.

"You can stay," I tell him, my voice coming out softer than I mean it to.

He nods, standing up and looking over my shoulder at my notes. "Can you play and sing that line again? I think I have an idea."

Sebastian sings against me this time when I play. The harmony he chooses fills out the sound so well and I want to cry with how much better it sounds.

"That sounds amazing," I tell him as I jot it down in my notes. "God, I'm so shit at this. You came in here and made this better in like two minutes than I would've in hours."

His hand rests on my shoulder briefly, before he quickly pulls it away. "I wouldn't have had anything to work on if you hadn't written it in the first place. Don't be so hard on yourself, Flora. You make great music already, and you will continue to make even better music. Let it happen."

Sebastian moves around behind me. I turn to see him picking up a guitar and move back in his seat.

"Play me what you have so far, from the start. Talk me through it and I'll add in what I can."

***

We end up working for a couple hours. It's all business, but I did catch myself staring at him sometimes.

When he pushed up the sleeves on his Henley shirt before playing. How he tied back his hair before writing in my notebook. How he then placed the pencil in his teeth to try something new on the guitar again.

It's intoxicating.

Chapter 14

I zone out, watching the coffee machine drip little drops of my sanity into a cup. Drip by drip, it falls so slowly.

I run through last night again. It was so good to work through that song with Sebastian. I think even he enjoyed it. When we finished up for the night, he asked me for my number and we've been exchanging the odd text here and there today. Different ideas for what we could do with the song.

I take out my phone, leaning against the counter as the slow ass coffee machine continues its hard work. I scroll through the texts we've sent so far, a little smile playing on my lips.

The song was in pretty early stages when Sebastian came to me, so it will still take a bit of time before it's actually finished. I wonder if he will want to keep working on it together. I decide to be brave and text him to ask:

I don't feel like it's only my song anymore. Do you want to keep working on it with me?

I slip my phone back into the pocket of my strawberry embroidered jeans. I grab my coffee cup and add a little creamer before turning to assess the break room.

One aspect of the new studio has been getting to learn a new routine. And I still haven't decided where the best place to take my coffee break is yet.

Oh, there's Tabitha, her lovely long blond wig on full display. It took a bit of finagling to get it to fit her head properly, but I put time into helping her out and smuggling her products from human territory. She looks great, the blond making her green skin pop.

I move over to her and we chat a bit. She tells me the latest gossip about a pair of orcs in finance who have been fighting over the affections of one of the human administrators. Neither of them have seemed to realize that the human isn't into either of them at all, but a quiet little deer shifter.

"Oh my God, stop! They're going to freak when they catch on," I laugh with my new friend. She works in admin, so she kind of does a bit of everything for everyone. Which suits her perfectly, being the huge gossip that she is.

I take a sip of my coffee, and then nearly spill it all over myself when my phone vibrates on my butt. Setting my coffee down, I whip out my phone quickly, hoping it's a message from Sebastian. It is:

I'm glad you asked, I was hoping you would. Do you want to stay late tonight and work on it?

"Ugh, let me guess, *Sebastian* is texting you," Tabitha giggles. "You have that lovesick little grin on your face."

I blush a little, choosing not to reply to her on the matter. I text back:

Meet you in Studio 1 again? Say 7:30 pm?

I hear the sad coffee machine again and turn to see who its next victim is. It's Sebastian. I watch his face light up as he smiles at his phone. I wonder if it's me he's smiling like that for.

He turns and catches my eye. He holds up a finger, and a moment later he's bringing his coffee over to join Tabitha and I.

"I assumed you'd be busy right now, that's why I had suggested this evening. But if you're free I can see if there's an available studio for the afternoon?"

He gives me a courtesy side hug in greeting, to keep up appearances. When his lips brush my cheek, I certainly do *not* squirm a little in my seat.

"Yeah. Alex isn't around today, so I was going to work on my own. I already have Studio 1 booked in ten minutes."

"Perfect."

"Well, I actually have to head back to work now. But you two lovebirds enjoy each other's company." Tabitha calls as she walks away from the table.

"It's nice to see you've made friends with some monsters," Sebastian says, taking a sip from his coffee. "You're settling in well with the changes?"

"Yeah, it's really nice actually." I look around the room, observing how all the different groups are a mix of humans and monsters. All it took was a bit of open-mindedness and a willingness to look past our differences. How they have all integrated so well together. Even with some new office romances in tow. Maybe soon they won't need a fake couple like Sebastian and I.

For some reason, I find that I really don't like that they could just call the whole thing off.

Chapter 15

"How do you want to start?" I ask, setting my bag down on the sofa in the back of Studio 1. "We could lay down what we came up with yesterday, to start?"

Sebastian looks a little confused, staring at all the knobs and dials on the mixing board. Ah, so he's not super technical then.

I giggle at him as I switch on the computer.

"This is a good place to start," I whisper.

"Do you know how to do all this?" He asks me, a surprised note in his voice.

"Enough to get us through decently, as long as you're not expecting it to be some avant garde techno piece. I took a few music tech classes in college."

He huffs, and I maybe think he's impressed?

I sit down at one of the producer's chairs, plugging in a flash drive to the computer and setting up a new project on the software.

"Can you hop in the sound booth so I can check all the hookups?" I ask Sebastian, taking charge of the studio.

He follows my orders so nicely, going through each step I ask before joining me at the desk again.

"I think there's a cable disconnected under the desk." I move to climb under, but Sebastian stops me.

"Don't worry, I can do it." He crawls under before I can stop him. "What am I looking for, boss?"

I laugh at the sight of this massive monster male crawling under a desk and calling me boss.

"OK, I'll bite. There's a MIDI connector that needs to go into a port labeled 2A. You got that?"

"I've found the port." He grunts, shifting around a bit, "If I was a MIDI cable, what exactly would I look like?"

Oh my God, the male is useless... I crawl under the desk to do it for him.

"Here!" I exclaim, finding the MIDI cable easily. "Just plug that into the port for me, please."

I only ask him because he's closer. But I stay to watch him, making sure that he doesn't fuck it up somehow.

Once it's all connected, he moves to get up, scooching back a bit and moving to stand.

A loud crack sounds, and I realize too late that it's his head hitting the table. I instantly move to make sure he's OK. I shift closer as he sits back on his ass. I push his hand out of the way and lean forward, examining where he hit.

"Well, you didn't break skin, at least." I tell him, gently brushing the reddening spot with my thumb. "You're really not good at the whole producing stuff, huh?"

He chuckles, shaking his head. I grip his chin, stopping him.

"Hey, no moving for a sec. Let's make sure you're OK first."

I run through a few concussion tests before I make the assessment that he's alright. It's one very useful skill that I picked up from dance.

I hold his face gently, and I can't help but laugh at the situation. He starts to laugh with me, and before I know it we're both tearing up with laughter.

My eyes lock with his and all of a sudden, I'm not laughing anymore. My breathing hitches, my hands still on his face. His face, that's so close to mine. I trace my finger over the scales on his cheekbone. It's even more interesting than I remember.

Sebastian reaches behind me, stroking the hair down my back gently. I shift even closer still, our breath mixing now. I could lean that extra inch or two forward, I could do it. His hand fists in my hair, his grip tightening slightly. I look at his eyes, but they're focused on my lips as he leans forward.

I turn my head quickly, pushing away and standing up. I try to hide my heaving breaths as I brush my jeans off.

"God, it's really dusty under there." I pick off a piece of lint from my t-shirt. "You'd think it wouldn't have gotten like that so quickly. It's only been like a few weeks since they built the damn place."

I turn around, moving to the computer to check our cable worked the way I thought it would. Sebastian has stood up now, his grumpy demeanor back in place.

"You know, I'm going to go use the restroom. I'll be back in a few." He says, not looking at me. Getting up and leaving the room quickly.

I let out a huge sigh and put my head in my hands. What is wrong with me? My phone dings with a text from Frank:

Date tomorrow. It's another awards show, red carpet. Sebastian's nominated for his last album. Car will pick you up at 5 pm.

Well, that puts things right back into perspective for me. This whole thing me and Sebastian have is fake, and I'm letting it get to my head. Letting him kiss me would have been a mistake.

When he comes back, I act super professional. I show him how to take the recordings and then I hop into the sound booth and lay down the piano and some of my vocals.

We switch places and then I do the same for him. Afterwards, I lay it all together as Sebastian sits on the couch and listens. We make sure not to touch or go near one another for the rest of the session.

Chapter 16

The dress that's been chosen for me tonight is ethereal. The thin wispy layers of tulle are divine. A single sheet would be see-through, but the layers give it opacity. Plus, it's lined on the bust. The dark raspberry color makes my skin glow, especially as it dips into a low 'v' between my boobs.

I twirl a little, watching the sparkles shift in the light. I'm waiting in the lobby of my building, yet again. I feel like whenever I have the team to get me ready, I'm always done way too early. But maybe that has more to do with the fact that my clothes are chosen for me.

When the car finally arrives, I get in quickly. I want to chat to Sebastian quickly about what happened yesterday, put it all behind us. Except it's not just Sebastian in the car, Matilda is back.

"Oh, hi Matilda!" I sit next to Sebastian. Noting that surprisingly he is sat next to where I normally do. Clearly, the days of sitting as far away from me as possible are gone.

"Hey," I say, just for him.

"Hello, sunshine." He smiles and it's incandescent. "You look great. I really like this dress on you."

I'm sorry, who is this male? I blush at his words. He looks great too, in his usual red carpet tux.

"So!" Matilda interrupts our intimate vibe with her chirpy voice. "We're going to need another shot for socials today."

She directs us through the motions, like before. This time around, Sebastian is cupping my face and leaning down like he's about to kiss me. I'm gripping his lapel lightly, my breath heaving, just waiting for the moment to be over.

"Perfect!" Matilda scoots away, scrolling on my phone and making the edits for the post.

Sebastian delicately extracts himself from me. "Sorry about that." He gives me a little space, but still stays on the same seat as me.

"So," I clear my throat slightly. "My manager told me that you're nominated for an award tonight?"

"Oh, yeah." He runs a hand through his hair. "It's for 'Album of the Year', but I don't think I'm going to win it though."

I blink at him slowly. "This is only for monsters?"

He nods, resting an arm on the back of our seat.

"Have you won it before?" I ask, realizing that he has five albums. This might not be his first time winning this award.

"Umm... yeah, I have."

I roll my eyes, "How many times?"

"Three." He smiles, bashfully. "I didn't get it for my debut album."

I slap him lightly on his shoulder. "Then you deserve to win it for this album too. It's arguably better than your first four, in my opinion."

He smiles to himself, preening under my compliment. I can't help but join him in the smile too.

"So, are y'all dating for real, now?" Matilda quips, staring at us from the other end of the car. I had sort of forgotten she was there for a moment.

I freeze, not sure what to say. Sebastian steps in and saves the day, though.

"That's hardly an appropriate question, Matilda."

She hangs her head a little and goes silent. Normally I would feel sorry for her. But Sebastian is right, it *was* an inappropriate question for her to ask. It also ruined the easy going tone we had.

We pull up to the venue at last. Sebastian climbs around me to be the first one to leave the car. He holds out a hand for me and gracefully assists me in getting my dress free.

We pause for photos before making our way into line for the red carpet. I think it's expected now that if Sebastian is invited to an event, I will be joining him. The initial shock from our first two appearances is long gone. It all feels kind of normal.

Sebastian keeps his usual hand on my lower back as we move through the line. But he's also a bit more handsy than normal. He's quick to fix a stray hair back into place, or smooth down my dress when the breeze gets under it.

When we get to our markers on the carpet, he bends down to fluff out my skirt for me before we pose. He's so attentive throughout the evening, doting on me and making sure that I have everything I could possibly need.

He wins his award, and my heart is full when I watch him give his acceptance speech. Addison joins him for the acceptance, a stunning navy blue gown draped over her plush form.

Sebastian insists that he doesn't want to go to an after party, award or not. He just wants to see me home and then go to bed.

I must doze off on the car journey back to my place because I am woken by Sebastian gently nudging me.

"Hey, sunshine. You're home."

I nod absently, getting up and making it into my building. In the elevator up I have a thought, did I fall asleep on him? I don't think I even really noticed in my sleepy state.

I'm in my apartment for a couple minutes when my phone dings with a text:

Did you get into your apartment OK? You were very sleepy...

I send him a quick reply letting him know I'm home safe and sound. I take off my dress and climb into bed with my makeup still on.

Chapter 17

We're messing around in the sound booth again tonight, getting deep into the songwriting. The song is coming together though.

I'm seriously impressed with Sebastian's guitar skills. His hands are so big that he can pretty much play anything he wants on the instrument. I'm only extremely jealous.

We harmonize on different lines together and I record all of it. I'm sitting at the mixing desk, playing back the parts we've recorded, and I'm surprised at how well our voices sound together. We both have pretty low ranges, and the richness of our two sounds creates such a lovely timbre.

It gives me an idea, so I hop up, moving back into the sound booth. "Come on, I wanna try something on the guitar."

I drag him into the booth with me and pick up the guitar. I sling the strap over my shoulder, not bothering to sit. I ask him to give me a second to figure it out. Then I play a little riff that I had in mind.

"Oh, I like that." He listens, closing his eyes as I play it again. "Try moving your fourth finger up to the fifth fret on high 'e' and see how that sounds."

I try what he asks, laughing as my finger is nowhere near long enough to hit the fifth fret.

"I physically can't do that." I really do believe he is oblivious to how small my hands are compared to his.

"Sure you can!" Sebastian moves behind me, I rest my arms as he plays around me to show what he means. His warmth envelops me, and I try to focus on what he is doing instead of leaning into that feeling.

"I know what you meant, I just can't physically do it." I shove his hand aside and show him how pathetically far my finger will actually go. He tugs on it for me, seeing if he can stretch it out that way.

Sebastian burst out laughing. "OK, I'm sorry. You were so right, your hands are..."

I look up at him, turning a little. His words fading off as I stare into his bright green eyes. Sebastian leans forward, and I think that I'm going to let the kiss happen this time. I'm ready for it.

Except the bastard pulls away, clearing his throat. I slip the guitar over my head, frustrated that we have failed at this yet again. I don't even know why we are fighting this anymore. Everyone already thinks we are dating, we spend most of our time together, why not try it for real?

I grip Sebastian's hand, pulling him back to me. I set the guitar on the stand so I can give him my full attention.

"Why are we fighting this?" I ask him, simply.

He looks conflicted at my words, his hands trembling as he lifts them to cup my face. I close my eyes briefly at the contact, a sigh escaping me.

"I don't know..." his voice is a soft whisper. I open my eyes to see his are much closer than before. The glowing orbs searching mine.

His lips brush mine gently, and my eyes flutter closed. It feels like coming home after being away for an eternity.

"*Sebastian,*" I sigh into his mouth.

His hands pull away from my face and I almost whine at the lack of contact. Until they grip my waist, easily lifting me up off the floor. I wrap my legs around him and my skirt rides up. Sebastian grips my bare ass as he pulls me to him.

This time when we kiss it's on another level entirely. His kisses are voracious, and I let him take charge. He pushes me against the wall, the foam of the acoustic panels pressing against me.

I cup his face in one hand, as my other grips his hair tightly. God, I have been dying to touch Sebastian's hair like this for so long now. His teasing tongue gently parts my lips and I melt against him as he thrusts it into my mouth.

He grinds his hips against mine, and I can feel the hard length of him pressed against me. I gasp at the friction, and he pulls back slightly to check that I am OK. I lean forward and kiss him again, grinding against him more. It feels phenomenal, the hard pressure on my clit and the butterflies in my stomach from our kisses are almost too much.

Sebastian pulls away, pressing his forehead to mine and giving me a chance to take a breath. My chest is heaving and I feel a little lightheaded. I giggle softly, and he joins me. He shifts me slightly, so that only one of his hands is holding me up. His newly freed hand tucks some of my hair behind my ear and then he caresses my cheek.

I stroke my hands through his hair and we just smile at one another. I feel dazed, in a dreamlike state. I'm almost worried that I'm going to wake up and see that it's all been a dream. But the solid weight of him pressed against me assures me that this is no dream.

"We're both idiots," I tell him, smoothing a hand down his chest. "I am so sorry for not doing this sooner."

Sebastian smiles, kissing me again, like he can't quite believe it's real.

"Are you hungry?" He asks me. "I'm not ready to say goodbye to you tonight yet. And I'm sure you're going to need to eat dinner soon."

"I could eat." I stroke his hair, my hand wandering to trace the scales on his neck. I love being able to touch him freely like this.

I realize that we can't exactly go to a restaurant together. Hmm... I'll take him back to my place. Maybe I'll even be able to convince him to stay the night.

Chapter 18

We decide that driving our own cars to my place makes the most sense.

Sebastian walks me to my car, opening my door for me and buckling me into my seat. He kisses me slowly, and I savor every second. I feel like I've done some pretty good drugs, my heart light and my head spaced out. Driving probably shouldn't be on the cards right now.

He eventually pulls away, gesturing to his truck and saying he will follow close behind me.

I try not to speed on the drive home, but the dial does go over the limit quite a few times. Sebastian's truck is close behind me the whole way. I'm embarrassed to admit how much I have to stop myself staring at him in the rear view mirror, trying to keep my focus on the road.

I can't believe that we actually kissed. Are we actually trying this? I won't bother him about the details tonight, but I do want to clarify what's going on here soon, set some parameters. I hope that he's into the same things as me in the bedroom. Heck, I'm getting way ahead of myself. We've just kissed, a *very* hot kiss, all the same. But that doesn't mean he's going to hop into bed with me right away. God, I wish I had asked Tabitha or someone what the deal with monsters is. Are they more or less free, sexually? Do they like to wait and date for a bit, first?

It's both the longest and quickest drive I've done from the new studio so far. The anticipation is too much, and there's a wetness pooling in my panties. It's just dinner, I remind myself. I need to calm down a little. Pulling into my space, I stay in my seat for a minute and take a few deep breaths.

My rear view mirror shows Sebastian leaving his truck and walking towards me. Fuck, he is hot, his biceps look ready to burst out of his Henley shirt. He looks so good in that with his jeans, almost as good as he looks in his sweatpants.

I get out of the car when he approaches my door. He slams it shut behind me and pushes me against it, bending to kiss my neck. Oh, fuck. He moves one of his legs between mine and I unabashedly grind against it. His hand slips into my hair, gripping it tight and pulling me against his leg harder. My body is pressed flush against his, the hot pressure of him against me. I let out a little moan and he groans, moving to kiss my lips.

The kiss can only be described as a claiming. I'm helpless to do anything but kiss him back and grind against his leg. I whimper when he pulls away, wanting to drag him back down to me.

"Shh..." he strokes my hair, stepping away slightly. "I can hear someone coming."

A moment later, one of my neighbors walks to their car. He moves faster when he spots us, fear driving him into his vehicle as quickly as he can. He revs his engine and speeds away.

"I think you might have given him a bit of a fright," I giggle, patting Sebastian on the chest.

"God, Flora." He groans my name, pulling me close against him. "That drive was *torture*. I wanted to be near you again."

Warmth spreads through my cheeks. "Let's go get some privacy, then."

We make it up to my apartment with only two brief kissing breaks. Which I think is quite the accomplishment, personally. Nervously, I open the door to my apartment, curious to what he will think of it. I'm also worried that I didn't clean up this morning before I left.

The coast seems clear, everything neatly put away. I turn to look at Sebastian, but he quietly clicks the door shut before moving past me. He has a little wander, looking at my fake plants, my fresh flowers. He pauses a moment to have a closer look at my vinyl collection.

"Do you mind?" He asks as he pulls one out, moving towards the record player.

"No, go ahead." I'm still standing by the door, observing him. I twirl my key around my finger, "what do you think of my place?"

"I like it. It's cozy but also nice and airy. Does it get a lot of sunlight?"

I nod, hearing the opening phrase of my favorite Clarissa Raye album playing. I recall a brief memory of telling him it was my favorite after the club, when we were talking about music the first time.

Sebastian wanders into the kitchen area, opening the fridge.

"What are you doing?" I ask, tossing my keys in their dish and following him in.

"Cooking," he says, simply.

"Oh! I thought we would get takeout." He is going to be disappointed with whatever he finds in my fridge. Even I don't know what's in there right now.

"I want to cook for you." He reaches in, moving a few things around. "Where's your pantry?"

I open the correct cupboard for him, gesturing for him to go ahead. "You see, the thing is, I really *don't* cook. So I'm not sure if there even is anything you could make a meal out of."

"I can see that," he chuckles. "Lucky for you, sunshine. I'm pretty creative."

He picks through my cupboard, and I leave him to it. My kitchen is pretty small, and there's not much space in there normally. Never mind with a fully grown dragon shifter.

I slip around to the other side of the island and sit on one of the bar stools. Sebastian really is too big for my kitchen. He pulls a selection of things out of my cupboard before opening my freezer.

"How long have these been frozen?" He holds up a zip lock bag with freezer burnt chicken breasts in it. I shrug, I really have no idea. I did not remember that they were in there. "You're really testing me, Flora."

"Well, I didn't know that you were planning on cooking in here!" We both giggle at our predicament. "Don't worry about it. I have very good Chinese food on speed dial."

"No," he sighs, trying to place his hands on his hips and banging his elbow on the fridge door. He pulls an unopened bag of battered chicken chunks from the freezer. "Huh, these aren't expired. Listen, it's not going to be the best meal I ever cook you."

He pushes up his sleeves, and all I can think about is when did forearms become so sexy? Sebastian leans across the island, "but it's important for me to cook for you right now. It's a shifter thing, so just let me look after you." He kisses my forehead softly, slowly pulling away. Turning, he shows me his back as he sorts through the ingredients he's chosen.

"Besides, next time I'll have you around to my place and I will cook you something really great."

He's talking about me coming around to his place? I wonder what it's like. Where does a dragon shifter even live? I think about what I know, feeling like Sebastian would have a very sophisticated apartment. Maybe some sort of bachelor pad. I guess I'm going to find out soon.

I flip the vinyl when needed, and then I chill on the couch, my feet tucked under me as I scroll on my phone.

I only hear a few bangs and swear words coming from the kitchen.

"Dinner is served," Sebastian calls. I make my way over to him as he places two plates on my tiny dining table. "Hang on, I poured us wine too."

I look at my plate as I sit cross-legged on my chair. It looks like he's made some sort of mushroom risotto, with the chicken chunks on the side. Did I even have mushrooms?!

"I can see your confusion," he chuckles as he sets a glass of white wine down next to my plate. "I found a small jar of dried porcinis in the very back of your cupboard. They looked pretty fancy, so they were definitely a gift."

An astute assumption.

"You also had rice. The grain is a little long for risotto but it should be passable. I used some of your wine to cook that too. The chicken chunks are a little left field, I'll admit that. But you literally had nothing else to use as a protein."

I take a bite. He's so cute, watching for my reaction. It's actually pretty good, considering. "You did well. I'm surprised this managed to come out of my kitchen in its current state."

The wine pairs pretty well too, I decide, as I take a sip.

"I'm pretty into food," I tell him. "I've never been a good cook though, so I kind of stopped bothering after a while. My best friend, Rosie, and I used to live together and she cooked all my meals. Then when I moved into my own place, I started eating out a lot more and getting takeout."

"Well, we're a good match then." I cover my mouth to hide my smile, trying not to look too eager. "I love to cook. But tell me about Rosie, where is she at now?"

I tell him all about Rosie and our college experience as we eat. Mentioning her café now and how I will need to take him sometime, he needs to try her cooking. We spend the meal talking about that, and about my family. He asks follow up questions, and he's actually really chatty with me.

"Well," I set my fork down on my empty plate. "That was certainly the best thing that's ever been cooked in that kitchen."

"Then I am sorry to tell you, that is extremely sad." I laugh at his blatant teasing.

"I'm not going to lie, Sebastian. Until the night at the club, I really thought you hated me."

I nervously wait for his response, worried if I've put my foot in it.

"That couldn't be further from the truth, Flora." I look up to see the earnestness in his eyes. "I've been an idiot. I thought you wouldn't be interested in me, and I think

I internalized that a bit too much. Because I ignored any kind of sign you had given me. And then when I tried to kiss you the other day and you stopped it, I thought I had pushed you away...”

“You are an idiot, but I like you anyway.” I say, it's hard to believe what he is saying. But I'm not going to ask him to go into any more detail right now. I stand up and grab our plates. “I'm going to clean up real quick.”

I leave him to his thoughts and move into the kitchen.

I drain the sink, suds still on my hands as I finish up. I'm running them under the faucet when I feel Sebastian sidling up behind me. He lifts my hair over one shoulder as he presses his lips to my neck.

I moan, pressing back into his warmth as I rest my wet hands on the sink. He trails kisses up my neck before nibbling on my ear lobe. Before I know what's happening, he flips me around, lifting me to sit up on the island. I barely have the time to wrap my hands around his nape for stability.

Sebastian's mouth is on mine again and I lose myself to the kiss. I hook my ankles around his hips, pressing myself flush against him. My stomach presses against his hard length, so I rub against him as we kiss. His hands roam over my waist, my arms, and tangle in my hair.

He pulls away, nibbling on my ear and whispering, "I love your hair, sunshine. I've wanted to run my fingers through it like this for so long."

Sebastian strokes my hair, petting it and smoothing out any tangles.

"But I've also wanted to grip it like this, too." His hand tightens at my scalp, holding my head in place. Oh, fuck, my pussy gets so wet as he holds me there. "Do you like that, Flora?"

He continues his soft whisper in my ear, the deep timbre of his voice sending me. "Oh, fuck. Yes." I moan, grinding my hips and trying to get some friction.

"Good girl."

Sebastian kisses along my jaw, trailing a path to my lips. He controls my movements with his hand in my hair, all I can do is move my mouth and tongue against his. I fist my hands in his shirt and use my feet to push him even closer to me.

After a while, his hand relaxes, his kisses slowing and growing more tender. I just know that my lips are swollen from his attentions.

"We still have some wine left..." he smooths down my hair. "Let's go finish it before I head home."

He leaves the kitchen, grabbing our glasses and moving to sit on the couch. I slide down onto my feet, gravity working against me and I take a second to right myself before following him.

Oh, I am not letting him leave this apartment tonight. Let him think whatever he wants to.

I sit on the couch next to him, my feet tucked under me as I angle myself towards him. We drink wine and chat more. I make sure to touch him as much as I can. Resting my elbow on the back of the couch, I reach up and play with his hair as we speak. I make sure to let my skirt ride up, showing off my full thighs.

My brain is a little fuzzy, and I can't tell if it's because of the wine or the lingering effects of Sebastian pulling my hair and calling me a good girl. I am still shocked that he did exactly what I wanted him to in the moment. I wonder briefly if mind reading is a trait for a dragon shifter. Or am I lucky enough that he's into the same things as I am in the bedroom?

He finally finishes his glass of wine and sets it on the coffee table. Leaning towards him, I cup his face with my hand and kiss him. His hand roams down my back before settling on my ass and squeezing lightly. I kiss along his neck, following his move from earlier and whispering in his ear.

"I know you wanted to go home..." I nibble on his earlobe and he groans and squeezes my ass. "But I was thinking that it would be much better if you spent the night."

My teeth graze his lobe and I decide to add, "I want you to fuck me, Sebastian."

Chapter 19

Sebastian grips my chin, pulling me back to his mouth and kissing me deeply. He bites my lower lip and smacks my ass at the same time.

I cry out, the slap sending a pulse right to my clit.

"Do you like that, Flora? Do you like when I slap your ass?"

Whimpering, I nod as he smacks me again. I can feel the wetness pooling in my panties. Reaching down, I tentatively trail a finger along the length of his cock. He is *huge*. I've been with big guys before, but nothing like this.

When he doesn't move to stop me, I grip him through his jeans and squeeze. He groans into my mouth and smacks my ass again.

"Maybe it's time you take me on a tour of the rest of your apartment…" He suggests.

I eagerly stand up, pulling him with me. Taking him by the hand, I guide him back to my bedroom. I let go of his hand at the door, turning to face him. I slowly unbutton my shirt, watching him gulp as I slip it off over my shoulders.

"Your turn," I tease.

He quickly tosses his shirt over his head. Flashes of scales are spattered across his torso, but I'm not even looking at that. His torso is ripped, his abs far too toned for a musician.

I slide my skirt down over my hips, leaving me in only my panties and bra. He follows suit, slowly unbuttoning his jeans and sliding them off. I can see the outline of his cock in his boxers.

He snaps, moving forward and lifting me. I wrap my legs around his hips and grind against him. There's a texture there, the thin fabric of his boxers hiding nothing. I groan and grind against him again, loving the feeling.

Sebastian places me on the bed, unhooking my legs from around him and kneeling before me. He rests them on his shoulders instead. Settling his face between my legs, he looks up at me and keeps eye contact as he sniffs my panties. Holy fuck, why is that so hot?

He pulls aside my panties with a finger, "God, you're *soaked* for me, Flora." His finger strokes through my wet folds, "such a good girl for me."

The room spins as he rubs his finger over my clit, my head falling back against the bed.

"Good girl, just lean back and enjoy." He slides my panties down my legs and tosses them. "Now I can get a good look at you."

He spreads my legs, his breath a hot tease. I try to lift my hips up but he grips my legs tightly preventing me from moving.

"Such a pretty pussy... I can't wait to taste it."

Sebastian licks a long line up my slit before circling my clit. I cry out at the tease. I can't help but grab my boobs, gripping them through my bra as I lose myself in the sensations.

He circles my clit a few more times, until I almost beg him to suck on it already. Then he flicks his tongue over it and a flush of sensation pulses through me. He licks, sucks and nibbles on my clit until I am falling over the edge.

I reach down, gripping his hair.

"Sebastian," I pant, "S-stop. I n-need a seco-oh!" Another orgasm washes over me as he continues through my first.

He sits back on his ankles, a satisfied look on his face. I think I've short-circuited, all I can do is pant and moan.

Sebastian moves over me, stroking my stomach as I try to catch my breath.

"Breathe, that's it." I grip his arm, my breath slowly returning to normal. "You make the prettiest sounds when you cum for me."

I grab his head and pull him down to me, kissing him desperately. I can taste myself on his mouth and it makes me want him even more.

Reaching down between us, I slip my hand in his boxers. I stroke him, feeling the hard ridges of scales there. He breaks our kiss, panting, a groan escaping him.

"I'm not sure you're ready for me yet, Sunshine." Sebastian gently tugs my hand away. He reaches behind me, lifting me gently and unhooking my bra. I raise my hands above my head, he firmly grips them there. With his other hand he trails his fingers gently down my neck and chest.

"Will you be a good girl and keep your hands up there for me?"

I bite my lip and nod, his dirty talk getting to me. I'm still riding the high of my orgasms, but Sebastian gently teases my nipples. Sitting back on his heels, he looks over me.

"You are such a sexy little thing, sunshine." I close my legs tight and twist trying to give myself some friction. I keep my hands pinned in place above my head though, I follow orders well.

Sebastian gets off the bed, slipping off his boxers. He stands in front of me, giving me a moment to look over him. His body is covered in patches of scales, the glistening color of a black void in the darkness. The windows let in a little light from the street, the color of him shifting to green as he moves.

His cock has two patches of the scales as well. It's so much bigger than anything I've ever seen before. It's not just about the size though, the anatomy is different than what I'm used to too. There's a sort of bump at the base, slightly wider than the rest of him. I wonder what that's all about?

Palming his cock and stroking lightly, he looks down at me through hooded eyes. The glowing green being the only light in the room.

"You still good, sunshine?" He moves to come back onto the bed, but pauses while he waits for my response.

"Hell, yes." I laugh at my own eagerness. I want his cock inside me, I want to feel him stretch me out. His face briefly shows a little relief as he moves onto the bed. Did he think he was about to turn me off?

"Can I please use my hands again?" I am eager to touch him, I want to run my hands over his dark skin and scales.

"Not yet," his fingers brush over my boob, squeezing lightly, before moving it closer to my core. "I have to get you ready for me first."

His hand dips between my thighs and they open for him greedily. I thrust against his hand as he strokes through my wetness. Sebastian dips one of his long fingers inside me and it feels so good.

"You're so tight." He leans forward, speaking right into my ear, the vibrations of his voice tickling in the best way. "Do you think you can handle me?"

"I have no fucking idea, but I'm going to try." I reply, grinding into his palm. "Fuck me with your fingers, Sebastian."

He takes his finger away quickly bringing it back with another one. He smoothly pumps into me and I can't help but thrust up to meet him. A slick sheen of sweat starts to cover my body, and I can tell that my hair is messed up. I can't bring myself to care as Sebastian gently sucks on my nipple, continuing to pump his fingers in me.

"Please, more..." I cry out as he slips a third finger inside me. It feels like I am full to the brim, the slight stretch so good. I can't wait anymore.

"I need your cock." He looks up at me, still tonguing my nipple. I nearly cum again at the sight, his mischievous grin as he bites down. I scream, straining to keep my hands in place. "Can I *please* move my hands?"

"Yes, you can move your hands." He chuckles as I fist my hands in his hair, bringing him close for a kiss. "You're such a good little girl, asking for permission."

Sebastian briefly lets me press my mouth to his, but it's not the claiming kiss that I need.

"Do you think I should reward you with my cock?"

I nod quickly, chanting "yes, yes, yes..." as he continues to finger fuck me into delirium.

Freeing his fingers from the tight grip of my pussy, he eagerly licks them off, one by one. "You taste so good," he says, lapping up what he can. It's filthily erotic and makes me even wetter.

He lifts my hips with one hand, grabbing a pillow with the other and shoving it underneath me. Sebastian kneels between my legs, fondling himself. He places my ankles on his shoulders, moving closer to me. Gripping his cock in his hand again, he moves it up and down through my folds, covering himself in my wetness.

Sebastian's eyes meet mine as he slowly enters me, my pussy stretching to accommodate his size. I fist the sheets under me with the effort of staying still. He pushes in a slight bit more and the stretch is almost painful now, the burn bringing me another wash of pleasure.

He reaches out, stroking my boob and flicking my nipple as he pushes in a little more. I grip his forearm tightly, breathing through the stretch.

"You're doing so good for me, sunshine." He looks down between us. "Look at that pretty pussy stretching wide for me…"

I cry out as he shoves in another inch. He settles then, staying still while I adjust. I don't have the patience for it, though. Thrusting forward, I take more of him in. I feel so full, stretched wide and full of his cock. My brain is a mushy mess and I become a pile of sensations, moving against him as much as I can.

He gets the message, pushing in the extra bit until it's just the swell at the bottom of his cock left. "We're gonna leave my knot for another time, OK?" I nod, not understanding much more than that this is as far as he is going today.

He pulls out slowly, maybe halfway before ever so slowly pushing in again. "Oh, fuck, Flora." I can see his skin glisten with a sheen of sweat. "You're so fucking tight."

He speeds up his pace and I see stars. Sebastian leans forward, testing the flexibility in my legs as they press against my chest. This angle hits me in just the right spot, and it doesn't take long for me to pulse around him. My orgasm crashes into me as I grip the hair at his nape tightly.

"Fuck yes, cum for me, Flora. Oh shit, yes." His thrusts speed up, giving me no rest as I crest into another orgasm. I can feel his cum spill into me, the warmth gushing. He fills me so much that it spills over and onto my sheets.

Sebastian releases my legs, and they fall open as he kisses me. His tongue explores me deeply, his cock still spurting cum inside me. Wow, I guess dragon shifters cum a lot. God, I do like it though. I feel so full of him.

I pant, trying to catch my breath as he releases me from our kiss. "That was..." I try to speak.

"Amazing." He finishes for me and I nod, agreeing, as I pull him back in for another kiss.

"Let me clean you up," he pulls away and I hear him potter around until he finds the bathroom.

All I can do is lie there as Sebastian comes back into the room and cleans me off with a damp cloth. He leaves and comes back again, this time bearing a glass of water.

"Come here," he slips an arm behind me and helps me up into a sitting position. He hands me the water and strokes my hair out of my face as I drink. I love how he dotes on me, making sure I use the bathroom and then tucking me into bed.

Sebastian climbs in under the covers a moment later and I laugh. "It's a good thing I'm a cuddler…" He takes up the entire bed. I push up and look, sure enough, his feet are hanging off the end.

He pulls me into him, calling me a brat and tucking my head under his chin. I snuggle into his chest, stroking the scales there until I fall asleep.

Chapter 20

I get into the elevator, laden with bags as I make my way down to the parking garage. Sebastian left already, but I didn't need to head to the studio quite so early today.

I'm giddy, a huge smile on my face as I remember the events of last night. It certainly wasn't what I expected to happen, but I am so happy that it did.

We didn't fuck again this morning, my pussy throbbing from being stretched out so much the night before. But boy did he make up for it, he went down on me again and I swear I have never met someone so skilled with their tongue. I squeeze my legs tight together now, just thinking about it turning me on far too much.

I shiver a little as the cold breeze of the garage hits me. Quickly walking over to my car, I pop the trunk and put my bags in. I've made up a little overnight bag to keep in there in case I have an impromptu visit to Sebastian's. I try to believe that I'm not totally delusional, but he mentioned like three separate times that he wanted to have me over.

"Slut!" I click my trunk shut and turn to see my neighbor from yesterday. The one who saw me and Sebastian at my car. "I had hoped this whole relationship with that *filthy creature* was all for the press. I know how you kids get stuck into awful kinds of contracts... but now I know better, you filthy monster fucking slut!"

I stand there, not sure what to say. This is an older man that I'm pretty sure I've helped with his groceries before. He's usually so sweet and kind.

"You should be ashamed of yourself." With that, he turns on his heels, making his way into the elevator.

I get into my car and lock the doors. What the fuck just happened? This is like Cian all over again... Why do people feel the need to push their hatred like this?

Trying to internalize whatever the fuck that was, I drive to the studio on autopilot.

I block out the experience entirely when I'm in the studio with Alex and Hyacinth. But I'm just running through the motions. I order us Poke bowls for lunch and I force myself to eat it. I made sure to order it from my favorite place to cheer myself up, but it doesn't hit the way it normally does. I barely eat half before putting the rest in the fridge for later.

Alex doesn't seem to notice there's something off with me. Or they do and they don't say anything. Either way, I'm more so being present for some post-production work. I don't even really need to be there.

Brightening, I think about the session I have booked in with Sebastian soon. Working on our song should cheer me up.

I don't follow Alex and Hyacinth out when we're done, sticking around for Sebastian. I don't have to wait long though, he comes in holding a tray with two cups of tea on it.

"Hey, Sunshine." He smiles, setting the tray on the coffee table. He sniffs the air gently, then turns to look at me properly. "What's wrong? What happened?"

I burst into tears, sobs wracking me, clearly waiting for someone to notice something was up. How does he know there's something wrong?

"Hey, shh..." he sits next to me and pulls me onto his lap. I cry into his chest and he strokes my hair until I tell him what happened in the parking garage.

"That little fucker..." Sebastian seethes, shaking his head. "I shouldn't have come to your place. I put you in danger... I didn't even think..."

"It's not your fault," I sigh and pick up my cup of tea. The hot liquid soothes my burning chest. "I don't even care about it really, I was just so shook by it. I was in such a good mood and he caught me at a vulnerable time. I don't care about the words of a bigot."

"I'm a bigot, Flora." Sebastian admits, running a hand down his face. I twist to look at him properly. "My family is as bad when it comes to humans. *I'm* as bad...

"I've always been raised to hate Humans, and I was forced into the whole PR thing with you. I didn't want to improve relations, I didn't care about them. But then when I met you and I didn't hate you... it made me so angry.

"So I refused to speak to you, only when I absolutely had to. I couldn't help but be drawn to you, though. I was attracted to you when we first met, and it kept getting worse."

I'm trying to see the positive here and not be insulted. Is he trying to say that he likes me in spite of himself? I'm trying to think through my other interactions with him, but there's never really been another human that he's been nice to. Well, not since we started working at the studio together. I've seen him chat with other humans... haven't I?

"What about now?" I ask him, my sniffling voice quiet.

"I've been so wrong," he chuckles. "First it was you. But then I met other humans, and I didn't hate them either. I liked your friends, and nothing crazy happened when we all started working together. And it made me wonder *why* I felt the way I did. Was it because of any actual thing? Or was it because it was how I was raised to feel?

"We're all people. And I regret how long it took me to get there."

I take another sip of my tea and then snuggle into him.

"I'm glad you're there now." I tell him. So many of our interactions make sense now. How he refused to look at or speak to me in the beginning. The way he's been slowly warming up to me.

I lean back to look at his face, tracing a finger over his jaw before kissing him. It's a gentle, simple touch of our lips. But I hope it conveys how I am feeling. I'm proud of him for opening up to me about that, it had to have been hard.

"We have work to do," I tell him. Standing up and downing the rest of my tea.

***

We spend hours working in the studio together, and we get a lot of work done on the song.

We also decide that it's just for us, that we don't plan on releasing it. We can have this one thing between us that has nothing to do with the label.

I'm working on a few edits, but of course another wire has come loose somewhere. I know better than to ask Sebastian to fix it, so I climb under the desk myself.

"Is it responding?" I call up as Sebastian checks the levels.

"Yeah, it all looks good." I turn to see him staring at my ass. What a perve...

I chuckle, turning around and kneeling in front of his legs. Sebastian groans at whatever he sees in my eyes.

"You look so good on your knees for me..." his voice trails off as he shifts in his chair and adjusts himself.

I reach forward, placing my hands on his knees and spreading them wide so I can slot between them. I slowly stroke up his thighs before I unbutton his jeans and take out his already stiffening cock.

Shifting closer, I lick him once from base to tip, my tongue tingling at the change in texture between his skin and scales. A tiny bead of pre-cum forms on the tip of his head and I suck it off, earning a groan from Sebastian above me. I continue sucking his head, my hands teaming up to stroke his length as I do.

Sebastian grips the arm rests on the chair tightly, holding himself back. I continue to tease him a bit longer, but he doesn't allow me more than that. The chair scoots back as he reaches down and picks me up from the floor. He pulls me onto his lap, shoving my dress up and my panties aside. He sinks into me quickly and I have to cover my mouth to hold in my moan.

"You naughty girl," he smacks my ass, holding tightly to not make a sound. "Do you think you can get away with teasing me like that?"

"Uh huh," I nod with a smile curling my lips. I lift myself up and down on his cock, fucking myself on him.

He meets my every thrust before gripping my hips still and speeding up. He thrusts up into me, and I hold him tightly as I orgasm. It's a quick relief, and he doesn't cum as much this time.

Sebastian rolls the chair back, grabbing some napkins from the table and cleaning us both off before we make too much of a mess.

I cry out a little in disappointment as he lifts me off him to clean us both better. I wish I could keep him inside me forever.

Pushing my panties back into place, I pull my dress down again. Then I take my seat and continue where I left off on the song. I smile to myself, hoping that it drives him a little crazy.

It's pretty late in the evening when we finish up in the studio. The song is almost ready, it only needs the final touches now, but we'll do that the next time we're in.

I'm packing my things away in my purse when Sebastian leans over me, speaking in my ear.

"I don't want to let you go, Flora..." He toys with my hair as he talks. "Will you come stay with me, tonight?"

"Two nights in a row?" I tease, knowing full well that I was about to ask him the same.

Chapter 21

The monster side of the city looks similar in some ways, but so different in others. I'm able to see everything, seated in the front seat of Sebastian's truck.

I can tell that we're in a nice part of town. We're currently driving through streets of pretty town houses, all with their own modifications. A selection have rooftop terraces, others have elaborate water features or fire pits.

Sebastian tells me that they are all a symbol for what type of monster lives there.

He switches gear, his hand coming to rest on my thigh as we go down a bit of straight road. "And this is my place." He squeezes my leg and lets go, turning into the drive of one of the town houses.

We pull right into a garage, the door closing behind us. I did catch a glimpse of the outside though. It was the biggest on the street, from what I had seen, three floors tall I think. Dark brown brick and an industrial looking black metal. This is all certainly a far cry from the bachelor pad apartment that I had been expecting.

Sebastian gets out of the truck, opening the back to grab my bags for me. I hop down too and take stock of my surroundings. It's a neat space and pretty bare. There is a steel shelving unit with some boxes, but overall I can safely say that he's not a car guy. There are no tools or grease stains to be found.

The door from the garage leads us through a laundry room and then into a hallway off his kitchen. His kitchen must be as big as my entire apartment. There are sleek black cupboards and clean marble counters.

The ceilings are high and the furniture is all a little bigger than I'm used to. I guess that makes sense. I remember how huge Sebastian looked in my little kitchen and I giggle to myself.

"You're making me nervous," he says as he sets my bags down. "Why are you looking at my kitchen and laughing?"

"It's called getting a taste of your own medicine." I sidle up to him, my hands on his chest. "You were so weird, looking around my apartment. And if you have to know, I was remembering how huge you looked in my kitchen. This one suits you much better."

He leans down and kisses me, his hand on my waist.

"Speaking of my kitchen, we should probably eat something."

I look at the clock, it's far too late for dinner, but I also have barely eaten anything today. My stomach groans loudly.

"Well, your stomach agrees with me, at least."

"It's so late, I feel like my eating habits are all over the place at the moment. Maybe I'm becoming nocturnal," I giggle. "Are you nocturnal, is that it?"

"Flora!" He over exaggerates acting offended, hand on his heart. "Do you know nothing of my kind?"

I giggle again as he leans forward, trapping me against a counter.

"I'm a dragon, Flora, not a weird little *lizard*... Of course I'm not nocturnal."

"*Sebastian*," I try to add my own dramatic flair. "I have absolutely no idea what you mean, or why we're talking about lizards. But to answer your question, no. I actually have no idea about your kind. A crash course would be great, thank you."

"Is that so?" He lifts me up to sit on a high bar stool and kisses me. "I'll tell you whatever you want to know while I cook."

He does. Sebastian potters around his kitchen, looking every bit at home. A glass of wine is placed next to me, and as I sip I feel brave enough to ask him questions.

"So, why the lizards?" I tease, taking a sip of my wine. The berry taste bursting on my tongue.

"That's a common misconception, and an insulting thing to call a dragon. Because dragons are not reptiles, we're mammals."

Sebastian pulls out a deep pot and brings some water to a boil. "What do you know already, Flora? It might be good to know what we're starting with."

"Embarrassingly little," I admit. "My manager sent me a text at one point to tell me that you were a dragon shifter. That was all, no context. And that was after me begging for any kind of information before we signed up to the whole PR thing. I tried doing some research online too, but that was a dead end."

His hand falters, the pot lid making a crashing sound as he sets it down. His jaw is tight and he's gripping the counter hard.

"I'm sorry, did I say something wrong? Are you mad?" I ask, worried that I've fucked something up.

"I'm not mad at you, sunshine." He relaxes a little, turning to face me. "I'm just really angry that no one ever prepared you for *anything*. They took advantage of my m—" He cuts himself off, not finishing what he was saying.

I wasn't taken advantage of, was I? I think back over the fashion shoot and the PR stunt. I was given a choice on both things... or was I? It was always assumed that I would do as I was told, that I would get there eventually. I take a bigger sip of wine, wishing I hadn't thought about this too deeply.

"Sorry, I'm angry *for* you, not at you. And I don't want to ruin the mood." He pulls out a chopping board and gets started on what looks like a salad.

"No, it's good for me to think about..." I sigh, kicking my legs back and forth. "I hadn't thought about it like that before. But you're right, no one ever really prepared me for anything..."

Sebastian appears before me, his hand cupping my cheek. "I'll look after you now. I'll tell you whatever you want about my kind, about the monster world."

I smile, nodding up at him and I realize that I believe him. I trust him with this.

"How about I show you more about the dragon stuff after dinner? It's definitely more of a show and tell kind of thing..."

I grin, excited about the prospect.

***

Sebastian makes the most delicious meal. It's a seared tuna steak with this really nice puree and a green bean salad. It's light and refreshing, and I don't feel too full afterwards.

"I'll take you up to the roof to show you all about how my abilities work in a little bit. But before then, there's another conversation that I would like us to have while we're in a more relaxed setting."

We're sitting at one end of his dining table across from one another.

"Oh, OK. What is it?"

"We kind of got a bit into it and carried away last night. But we probably should have chatted about our limits beforehand. What we both like in the bedroom…"

I squirm a little in my seat as he looks across at me. His head resting on his folded hands and I feel prized under his gaze.

"Do you want me to go first?" Sebastian asks.

"Umm… no. Can I go first? I always feel awkward going second with these kinds of chats." His eyebrows raise at my response. Did he think I wouldn't have had a conversation like this before?

"Of course, go ahead."

"I want to start by saying that if you're not into any of the same things as me, that's OK, it's not a deal breaker for me. I'm open-minded, and I will try other things... I just happen to know what I like." I take a deep breath, letting it out slowly.

"I'm sure you picked up on it last night, but I'm a submissive. I'm not a brat, really. I might have fun sometimes, but I always do as I'm told, it's what makes me feel good."

"I did notice," he grins, his teeth showing a little.

"And I like it when... I like a little pain, but it's more the control aspect. I like to be manhandled a little bit, to be put in my place. You can smack me, and move me around roughly... I really like that.

"I also love to be choked. I know not everyone is into that, and that's OK if you're not—"

"Oh, I am very into that." He lays a hand out on the table for me to hold. "Don't worry, sunshine. I am very much into the lifestyle. You're not going to scare me off. Tell me what you know you like, and what you'd like to try. Don't hold back, you can trust me."

"OK," I sigh, gripping his hand tightly. Staring at my empty plate, I continue. "So, yeah, I really like to be choked. I want you to take charge and fuck me roughly, pick me up like a doll. I'm really into being praised too, I want to do as I'm told and be a good girl."

I bite my lip and look up at him. He is looking at me intensely, with approval in his eyes. I preen a little before continuing.

"I'm also really into being fucked while I'm asleep... just the thought of waking up and already being fucked or licked out makes me so wet."

"What about a safe word, do you have one already?" He asks, stroking his thumb over my hand.

"Yep. I use the traffic light system."

He moves to speak, but I cut him off.

"There's actually something else, something I've wanted to try." I steal myself before admitting it. "I've never found someone else who was into it, so it's OK if you're not. But... I've always wanted to be chased."

I look up at him, judging his reaction. Most people think this one is weird when I bring it up.

"I want you to clarify that a bit more for me."

"Umm... OK. So, I've had dreams like this before, and I think about it sometimes when I masturbate. I like the idea of being chased, like I'm being hunted, and that when I'm caught they'll fuck me. Even if I kick or scream at them to stop."

Sebastian gulps, "I know I said I would hold off on the dragon stuff for a little bit. But the predator in me would love to do that with you."

I try not to get too excited... "Really? You're not making fun of me?"

"Definitely not," he shifts a little in his seat. "I'm hard as a rock thinking about it."

That made him hard? Thinking about chasing me? Fuck, I need a fan, it is getting too hot in here.

"Let me tell you mine?" I nod, gesturing for him to tell me about his kinks.

"I'm not sure how much you will believe me now... You're right, going second sucks. But we're matched pretty well, Flora.

"For me, it's about the control, yes. But I don't take that lightly. I want to look after you too. To make sure you've received lots of pleasure, along with a little pain. But I'm not out to hurt you, either. I only use pain when I know the recipient is also into it.

"Controlling someone's breath is a big thing for me too. Not just choking in the traditional sense, but using my submissive's body how I please. That could mean I fill up your mouth with my cock until you choke on it too."

I can't help but cut in. "Yes, please."

We both laugh at each other. Just talking about this has made the room thick with sexual tension. I'm glad he chose to do it while we are sitting across a table from one another. Otherwise, I think I would be already fucking him.

"I am into everything else you mentioned, too." He squeezes my hand gently. "I'm sure constraints, like bondage are something that you're into too?"

"Actually, not really." I reply. "I want to be a good girl, like I said. So if you tell me to stay still or in a certain position, I want to prove that I can do it on my own."

"Fuck," he runs his hand through his hair. "You *are* a good girl."

I can't deal with him praising me like that, I can feel my panties getting wet. I know he's about to show me the dragon stuff too, I need to keep it together.

"What do I call you?" I ask him.

"Well, that kind of leads me onto the dragon stuff again." I shift forward in my seat, eager to hear what he means. "Did you know what my knot was?"

"I don't know that word apart from like, trying a rope? But I remember you saying something about it last night."

"The bigger part of my cock, towards the base. Do human men have that? Maybe they use a different name..." I shake my head at his question. "Oh, so you didn't know what it was?"

"No. But so much of you is different. I like it though." I don't want to insult him. "Is that your knot? What is it for?"

"Yeah, that's my knot. If I can fit it inside you, when I cum it swells up and locks us together. It's called knotting and it can last for a while..."

Oh, that sounds very interesting. I really like the idea of that.

"So you would stay inside me even after you cum?" I cross my legs , trying to create some friction without looking like it.

Sebastian agrees, "Which leads me to the name. I'd like it if you called me your alpha... it's a shifter thing and has to do with the knotting. Only alphas have knots."

"Oh, OK. I'll remember that." I decide to save my first time calling him alpha for when we're fucking later.

Chapter 22

Sebastian leads me out onto his rooftop terrace.

"It's time to teach you a little bit about dragons. If it's OK with you and you're comfortable, I can shift to show you." He suggests.

"Yes, definitely." I step out of the way, I'm so excited to finally see his other form. I've obviously seen his wings, but I think that there might be a bit more to it than that.

Sebastian takes off his shoes, before removing the rest of his clothes and putting them in a pile on a side table. His cock hangs heavy between his legs, and I have to hold myself back from moving to him.

"Are you sure you're comfortable?" He double checks with me before moving into the middle of the roof. "Make sure to keep back until I'm fully shifted."

Sebastian bends forward, his entire body shifting and stretching. His scaled patches grow in size and fuse together. Massive wings sprout out of his back as he continues to grow. His head shifts at the same time, a snout forming as Sebastian's face disappears.

An enormous scaled beast stands before me in a matter of seconds. While they are much bigger now, it's still Sebastian's glowing green eyes that look back at me. I can see his searching gaze as I move towards him. I touch the side of his snout, stroking softly.

"You're magnificent," I tell him. He huffs, steam escaping his nostrils.

The color of his scales shift in the moonlight as I make my way down his body, the light picking up his bright green. He stretches out his wings so that I can take a good look at them too. They are like a stretched membrane, so delicate that you can see the light through them. I reach out and run my hand over one. It's like the softest leather.

One thing I didn't see while he was shifting was his tail. I move around to it now, it's practically the same length as my entire body. There are spikes running down the length and it is tipped with an arrowhead shaped barb.

I'm amazed by him, moving back up to his head.

"You're incredible," I tell him, stroking along his snout again. I can't believe that this powerful monster wants to be with me.

He gestures towards his body with his head.

"What? Did I miss something?" Sebastian shakes his head no. "I don't understand... do you want me to climb you?"

He huffs, nodding his head lightly.

"Are we going to fly?!" I squeal as he nods his head again.

I assess his form, trying to figure the best way to climb him. There, his back leg has hard scales that stick out that I could almost use as a ladder. I climb up and settle between his wings. There are plenty of little pocket holds that I can use, so I grip his scales hard and let him know that I'm ready.

I wobble a little as Sebastian takes a step back, preparing to take off. I cling to him tighter, my legs squeezing hard. He spreads his wings and pushes up off the roof. He is smooth and steady, probably trying his best to stop me from falling to my death. I try not to think about that too much as we move higher into the sky.

It's a Friday night and the city is lit up. We're not the only people in the sky, but Sebastian keeps his distance from anyone else.

"The city is beautiful," I tell him. "It must be so nice to be able to come up here and fly whenever you want."

He nods smoothly. We watch the city for a bit, flying around in lazy circles.

"Can we go see my apartment?" I ask excitedly. But Sebastian shakes his head no. Instead, he flies further from Human territory. We speed up once we're over suburbs and park lands, until we're in the countryside. It's so peaceful, the only sound is our own breathing.

"I want you to take me here for the sunrise one day. I bet the fields would be lovely and foggy and so pretty."

After a while, the city lights form up ahead again and I disappointedly realize that we're heading back to Sebastian's roof.

Once we get there, I slowly climb off his back and move out of the way. Sebastian shifts back into his other form, and it's strange to see him like this and connect the two.

"I love flying!" I tell him, moving forward and hugging him. "Thank you for taking me out, it was so cool. And you're *huge* Sebastian, it's amazing."

He grins, "You really think so? I didn't scare you off?"

"I don't know where that is coming from, because this is so much a pro and not a con."

He blushes and it's adorable.

"So what else makes a dragon?" I ask.

"Fire," his eyes light up, the green glowing more intensely. Sebastian holds up his hand and a green flame appears there. "I can shift the shape, and throw it too. Dragons breath fire, but we're not permitted to do that in the city, for obvious reasons.

"I also couldn't bring you to your apartment when you asked because that's a no-fly zone. We can't fly in the human territory at all."

Oh, that makes sense. I can't imagine that going down well.

"I'm not going to lie, Sebastian…" I trail my hand up his arm. "I found the whole thing pretty attractive. You are so strong and capable, and you can *fly*."

I run my hands over his chest. Sebastian leans down and kisses me. His cock juts up between us, pressing against my stomach. I reach down and stroke him, paying special attention to his knot.

I see the surprise in his eyes as I pull back quickly.

"Catch me." I call. I grab his clothes and run back inside, shutting the door behind me.

Chapter 23

Sebastian doesn't immediately follow me, but I still need to move quickly to find his room.

I try a door, but the bedroom inside is quite plain and not lived in. So I figure it's a guest room. I dump his clothes on the bed, trying to throw him off my scent, maybe he'll think I'm hiding in here.

I try the other doors on this floor but they're not right. Glancing at the door to the roof access, my heart is racing. I run down the stairs onto the second floor as quickly as I can.

The next door I try is the correct one, Sebastian's scent permeates the air. The walls are covered with different treasures, signed guitars and vinyls. There are other things in lit up glass cases, like jewels and keepsakes.

I shut the door behind me quickly, deciding to strip down to my underwear. His room is a mix of muted browns, burgundies and jewel tones. Sebastian's bed isn't really a bed like I know it, it's recessed into the ground. It almost looks like just a pile of blankets and throw pillows. But when I step on it, there is definitely a mattress underneath it. I like it, I decide, it's very cozy.

Laying down on the bed, I wait for him.

Sebastian leaves me waiting, the anticipation driving me crazy. I dip my hand between my legs and I'm soaking, my wetness spilling out onto my thighs. I try not to outright touch myself, instead squeezing my legs together for friction. My heart speeds up even more as the door handle slowly moves down.

The door creeps open and Sebastian comes into the room. He is pure predator, his eyes glinting, cock standing upright. I'm admiring him when the lights go out. The room is pitch black, I can't even see his eyes glowing.

I can't see or hear him, and I feel like prey caught in a predator's nest. My heart is beating so fast I can hear it in my ears. A hand ghosts over my pert nipple and I whimper.

Sebastian pounces. I'm grabbed by the waist and flipped over onto all fours. I barely catch myself, my hand slipping on a silk cushion. My panties are torn open, the sound obnoxiously loud in the silent room.

There's no foreplay tonight. Sebastian sinks deep inside me, knot and all, bottoming out. The mix of burning pain and pleasure makes me cum around him instantly.

The chase was everything I had wanted it to be.

"Good girl..." he reaches forward and grabs my boob, squeezing. "Cumming all over my knot like that. Do you feel how well it fits inside you?"

"Yes, alpha." Sebastian groans, pulling me closer against him.

"Remind me what your safe word is, again?"

"Orange if I want to slow things down. Red if I want you to stop." He squeezes my nipple tightly, so I add, "Alpha."

There's no warning again. Sebastian goes from bottoming out and holding me close to fucking me furiously. He grips my hips and pounds into me, hard and fast.

I drop my elbows, grabbing a cushion and pressing my head against it. I'm sweating all over, my hair sticking to my cheeks and my neck.

"You're such a good girl, taking your alpha's cock so well." Sebastian grips my hair pulling my head back. "Aren't you?"

"Yes, alpha." I moan. Pleasure rolls through me as he grips my hair tighter. My mind drifts off to a peaceful, simple place. All that exists is my alpha and my pleasure.

Sebastian bottoms out in me again, this time I can feel his knot expanding just inside my opening. It stretches me further than I ever thought possible. The pressure of his knot bears down against my clit, creating a new type of pleasure. I orgasm again as he cums inside me.

He moves us so that we're laying on our sides, in a spooning position. Sebastian smooths my hair out of my face as I orgasm around him again. Every tiny shift is amplified a thousand times, my clit oversensitive from the pressure. At the same time, Sebastian is still pumping me full with his cum.

I feel so full, the stretch of his knot and his cock still rock hard inside me.

"You're doing so well, Sunshine." Sebastian strokes down my side as he pulls me flush against him in the nest.

We have calm moments where we can speak. Until one of us shifts lightly and then we're both cumming again. We talk about lots of things, Sebastian tells me about his earlier gigs and stories from the road. I tell him about how I got signed to Fortune Records, and meeting Frank.

Eventually, I fall asleep, still knotted tight to Sebastian. It's the most blissful feeling.

Chapter 24

When I wake up, my first thought is how incredibly horny I feel. I realize why pretty quickly.

Sebastian is still cocooned around me, but I'm laying more on my stomach than when I fell asleep. My nipples burn with the friction against the sheets as I am shifted. Sebastian's cock is already deep inside me, and he slowly eases himself in and out of my pussy.

There's something so tantalizingly taboo about falling asleep with his cock stuffing me full and then waking up to being fucked again. It takes me a few more seconds to wake up properly and register what was happening.

"Alpha?" I ask with a sleepy moan.

"Hmm…" he happily nuzzles my hair. "Good morning, pretty girl."

Sebastian strokes his hand down my body, beginning to circle my clit with a finger. He keeps up the steady, slow thrusting of his cock. I can feel how wet I am, his finger gliding easily through my folds.

"H-how long have you been f-fucking me?" I struggle to get my words out, the pleasure taking away my ability to do much.

"About ten minutes or so, I'd say…" I gush, feeling a hot surge of cum come from deep within my pussy. Sebastian groans, bucking a little before easing back into his steady rhythm.

My pleasure gradually builds again at a languid pace. My face is still sleepily smushed against a pillow as I sigh and moan at every small feeling.

Sebastian moves his hand away from my clit and I cry out at its absence. Until he brings it to my neck, circling me there. The feeling of his hand wrapped around my throat is far better than my clit. He adds a slight bit of pressure, testing me out.

"Please, choke me harder, Alpha." I slow my breathing as he squeezes me tighter. I wait through it, patiently letting him decide how much I can take, pressure filling my head. When Sebastian releases the pressure a little, I feel a wave of pleasure crest through me.

Two thrusts of Sebastian's cock later and I am crying out through my orgasm. I've lost count of how many times I've cum since entering this room.

My hair is pulled tight and I can't help but let my head be lifted up and to the side. Sebastian's face hovers over mine, then he leans in and claims my mouth with his. His cock is pressed deep inside me as his tongue explores my mouth. I can barely breathe in this position, my mouth blocked off. My head getting lighter as I lose myself in his kiss. I can see colored spots behind my lids by the time Sebastian pulls away.

My hair is still gripped tight as he smiles down at me. It's beautiful, his eyes are bright but his lids are drooped heavy with fatigue.

"You're doing so great," he tells me. Sebastian reaches down and pinches my nipple hard. It's exactly what I need, grounding me in the moment a little better. "I'm so impressed with how well you're taking me."

Sebastian kisses my shoulder, releasing my hair. My head would have flopped down onto the pillow, my strength completely gone. But he slowly eases it down for me, making sure I don't bang it.

"Are you going to be a good girl for your Alpha and take my knot again?"

You would think that I wouldn't be able to take anymore fucking, but I keep getting more and more aroused with Sebastian. I'm beyond words by now, so I nod and push my hips against his, trying to push his knot in for him.

He pushes me flat onto my stomach, lifting my hips. Sebastian fucks me hard again and I wonder where he gets the energy from. He's quick now, having teased himself enough with his slow movements earlier. I feel the moment when his knot pushes inside me and starts to expand again. An orgasm forces its way through me as the pressure builds against my clit again.

"A-ah, it's too much!" I scream, my loudest yet, as the pleasure really does start to become too much.

"You're doing so well, Flora." Sebastian uses my name, pulling us from the scene a little. "Do you need to use your word?"

I shake my head. "I d-don't want to stop. It's... oh—" I orgasm around him as he shifts onto his back, pulling me with him.

Sebastian strokes my hair, and caresses my body as I lie on top of him. He keeps his hips perfectly still as he does, careful not to shift me into another orgasm.

"Good girl," he soothes.

Chapter 25

I curl up in the blankets, turning over and breathing in the scent of clean linens. Judging by the lack of furnace next to me, I must be in the bed on my own.

Sebastian's bed looked strange at first, but now I totally get it. The piles of blankets and pillows are superior. The blanket laid on me right now feels freshly laundered. And now that I think about it, I feel a little cleaner. Sebastian must have wiped me down at some point.

I never could have imagined he would be so attentive. He helped me to live out all of my fantasies. I don't know what I did to deserve someone who matches me so well, but I'm definitely not going to let him go now.

Things had gotten so intense last night that I had kind of forgotten about his dragon form. He truly was amazing. Blushing, I think about how that beast is inside him while he fucks me. A flush of heat hits me, not in a sexual way, I'm just *hot*.

I toss the covers off, but it doesn't help very much. Climbing out of the comfy nest, I make my way over to the windows. I pull back the curtain and shove the window open. The cool breeze is incredible, my nipples standing up at the sensation.

The sun is up, but I would put it at late morning. The street below is calm, there are no other people about right now. If someone were to walk by though... they would see me up here, naked. Another flush of heat makes its way through me, and I notice how turned on I am. I didn't think I was much of an exhibitionist before. I moan, and in my lust filled haze I realize that I'm already rubbing my clit. Huh, that's weird. I don't remember doing that, but it feels so good. I pinch a nipple with my other hand, groping my boob. Another surge of heat fills me as I think again about how anyone could look up and see me right now. Eyeing up the deep window ledge, I wonder if it would feel good to grind up against it.

A sound startles me and I turn to see Sebastian setting down a tray of food. He's only wearing a pair of sweatpants, hanging low. His torso on full display like that has me rubbing my clit fast, pinching my nipple harder.

"Are you OK, Sunshine?"

I groan, my fingers slipping in my wetness. His voice is so deep and melodic, I want it to wash over me, I want to hear him whisper in my ear the way he does. Ugh, it feels so good when he does that.

"Flora?" He has a stern quality in his voice this time, and I pout, that's not what I wanted. "Are you OK?"

"I'm really hot," I whine. I can feel little droplets of sweat running down my back now.

Sebastian moves towards me and I whine as he pushes my hand away from my pussy. But then I sigh when he replaces it with his own.

"Let me help you with that," he says. Sebastian grabs my ass with his other hand, squeezing hard. A finger slips inside me and I start to grind against him. I grip his arms as I hump his hand, the friction delicious. But it makes me hotter, even still. I rest my head against his chest, but it's so hot. Everything is so hot.

His hand smooths my hair from my face. Sebastian pulls back a little, catching my eyes with his.

"Can you pay attention for a second, sunshine?"

I groan, grinding against his hand harder, struggling to claim my orgasm.

"Do you know what going into heat is?"

Biting my lip hard, I shake my head.

Chapter 26

Sebastian groans, kissing the bite on my lip.

"Concentrate for me," I want to do as he says so I look up at him. I slow my humping a little. "Good girl."

"There's more dragon stuff that I probably should have told you. I just didn't think that this would happen to a human. Going into heat is a side effect of knotting with an alpha."

"I'm so hot," I whine. "And I'm horny, Sebastian. I'm so hot and horny."

Sebastian kisses my forehead, gently.

"I can make it go away, I promise." He says. "Do you trust me?"

I nod, looking up at him and leaning up for a kiss. Sebastian leads me back to his bed, and I lay on top of the covers. He kneels before me, bending between my legs and licking my pussy. His fingers slide inside me and I grab his hair, grinding against him until I orgasm.

He continues licking me through it, fucking me hard with his fingers. It doesn't take long for another climax to burst through me. My body temperature goes down a bit. I'm still uncomfortably hot, but my horniness has subsided a little, at least.

"It will take a bit more than that to get the heat to subside." Sebastian tells me, coming up from between my legs. "That should do you long enough to have a little food."

He gets up and brings the tray from earlier to the bed. Before he lets me touch the delicious looking plate of cheese and fruit, he makes me down a huge glass of water. He's right though, I haven't drank anything in so long and I've definitely lost a lot of fluids.

I nibble at the food some, but I find that I don't have much of an appetite, after all. When I'm done with my plate, Sebastian picks me up and brings me to the adjoined bathroom. It's a stunning marbled room with brass hardware, the tub is huge too.

Sebastian sits me on the edge of the tub as he fills it with hot water, adding some salts to it too. There's a mass of hot, bubbly water now as he lowers us both into the bath. The heat is too much, and I pull away, trying to get out. He keeps me next to him, settling me on his lap.

"I know, it's hot. I promise it will help though." He strokes down my back, cupping the sudsy water and dripping it over me. After a minute, the water does start to feel nice. It's cozy, and I settle against him. I shift until I am straddling him. The scales on his cock feel amazing as I grind against them.

Reaching between us, I grab his cock and slide him inside me. Finally. It feels incredible to have his cock filling me. Sebastian groans, kissing me and wrapping his arms around me, holding me close. I ride his cock until I cum again, clinging to him as I ride it out.

"You're doing so good," He strokes my wet hair away from my face again. I feel like a mess, my horniness having returned in full force, that last orgasm making me want more.

Sebastian pulls out of me before he cums himself. I'm confused at first, but then I'm distracted as he massages my scalp with a floral scented shampoo. I close my eyes and groan as he cleans me all over. It's really nice to have someone wash me and take care of me.

He holds me in his arms as he stands up, a sheet of water falling off us. He sets me on the floor and wraps me in a soft, fluffy towel. I burrow in, enjoying the feel of the fabric on my skin. Sebastian quickly dries himself off and I can't help but reach out and take his cock in my hand. I stroke him and I start to bend so I can put him in my mouth.

"That's not going to help you with your heat." He grips my shoulders, pulling me back up.

Sebastian turns me so I'm facing the slightly foggy mirror, stripping me of my towel. He kisses my neck and palms my boobs. "Look at how beautiful you are..." he tells me. "Do you want to watch while I fuck you?"

"Yes, alpha."

He lifts my leg at my knee and sets my foot on the counter. I stretch into the position, my foot on the floor going on my toes and my hand supporting me on the counter.

"Look at that pretty pussy," he tilts my hips forward so I can see. I fall back a little but he supports me with his body. "Are you going to be a good girl and hold that position for your alpha?"

He's testing me on what I said yesterday. I get even wetter at the thought, I can hold this for my alpha.

"Green," I say. I grin at him in the mirror as I relax my head against his chest.

"Good girl." I preen under his praise, pleasure flowing through me at his words.

Sebastian bends slightly to accommodate our height difference. I watch in the mirror through heavy lids as he slides his cock inside me. Seeing it happen as I feel him is such a turn on. He pumps in and out of me, slowly at first. When he starts to pick up speed, he scoops up my leg at the knee again, holding it up for me. His other hand reaches around and grips my neck. He holds me there with pressure for a long time as he fucks me, my breathing limited to little sips of air. When he lets go, I cum with the force of the oxygen flooding my system. He holds still for a second as my pussy grips him tight.

Sebastian pulls his cock out, flipping me like I'm a doll and sits me on the counter. I'm still struggling to catch my breath as he kisses me deeply. He slips his cock back into me again, breaking our kiss to fuck me hard. I'm light-headed from all the sensations. His hand cups my head so I don't bang it against the mirror, his other holding my waist to keep me still.

"Look." He commands, pushing my head forward so I can see him pumping into me. I can see when he shoves that extra bit more and my pussy stretches around his knot. I cling to him, pressing close, as he expands inside me. Feeling his cum fill me like that is so good, I don't think I could ever go back to fucking a human now.

An orgasm racks through me, the pressure of his knot too intense. Sebastian kisses me through it. He jolts against me and impossibly, I feel him cum inside me again.

"Fuck," he rests his forehead against mine. "You're too tempting, little Flora. I meant to knot you somewhere a bit more comfortable."

He straightens, picking me up with him and walking into the bedroom. I tremble through a constant orgasm as he moves, the pressure and friction too much to give me a break. He chooses to sit on an armchair rather than make it the whole way back to the bed. I straddle his lap.

This time, I'm not a passenger during the knotting experience. It must be this heat thing, but I can't help but grind against him. I hump him through multiple orgasms, switching between kissing him and nuzzling his neck.

Sebastian talks me through the whole thing, telling me how well I'm doing and how I'm such a good girl. Eventually, my skin begins to feel cooler to the touch, I shiver as his knot deflates beneath me. So much cum spills out of me and into Sebastian's lap.

My thoughts start to become more coherent, and I think back with horror at my behavior. Oh no, I literally threw myself at him.

"Are you feeling better now?" Sebastian asks.

I blush, trying to pull away, embarrassed. He holds me by the elbows and presses me against him. His warmth is nice as another shiver overtakes me.

"You have nothing to be embarrassed over." He kisses my forehead gently. "Going into heat is a super natural thing. You have no idea how attractive that whole experience was for me. You are irresistible, Flora."

I glance up at him, blushing.

"Really? I mean…" I lean forward, dramatically whispering. "I was *humping* you. Like some sort of an animal."

"I'm into that, Flora. In case you haven't noticed… I'm kind of an animal, myself."

We chuckle, and I feel a lot better about it. He gives me the cheekiest grin and luckily, I appear to be all sexed out. My pussy staying completely calm.

"Oh, thank fuck." I say.

He slaps my ass, "You've definitely earned yourself lunch."

Sebastian gives me a shower this time, washing me all over again. It's so relaxing when he massages the soap into me, I don't think I've ever been this clean. He dries me off, and dresses me in one of his big t-shirts and a pair of my own panties. He even grabs my cozy, fluffy socks from my bag too.

As if I'm not cozy enough, he sits me on the bed between his legs and painstakingly blow dries my hair for me. I feel like a pet, being groomed and stroked.

Sebastian makes us lunch, and we spend the evening curled up on his couch together, watching TV and snuggling.

Chapter 27

S ebastian pulls his truck up in the parking lot to the studio. The sun has barely risen, but we're on a mission this morning.

I slept for most of Sunday, curled up with Sebastian, either watching TV or talking. Turns out I needed to recover after all that sex. Who knew?

I sneakily suspected that Sebastian was just as worn out. Although he looked after me like a queen, doting on me and making sure that I stayed hydrated.

We walk into the studio together, having to scan our ID cards to get in this early in the morning. Because we had such a good rest, we were up especially early. I'm feeling inspired to finish our song today.

***

The few hours that we spend in the studio flies by.

"I think it's done!" I squeal. I added the final touches and we had a listen back. There's no other changes I would make to it.

I turn to Sebastian, jumping with joy. He picks me up and spins me around, laughing along with me.

"Wow, I can't believe it's finished." He tells me. "Now I'm going to have to come up with another excuse to spend time with you."

I slap his arm playfully.

"We could always go out to celebrate," I suggest.

Sebastian's phone dings before he can respond. He reads his text carefully, his expression darkening.

"Fuck, Karl wants me to go out of town for the night to do a TV appearance..." He runs his hand through his hair.

"Oh, that's OK!" I tell him quickly, trying to hide my disappointment. "We can go out once you're back. I could probably do with being home for a bit on my own, anyway."

Sebastian sighs. He seems frustrated, more than he should be.

"I'm sorry, Flora." He pulls me close and kisses me. I sink into the kiss and lose myself in it for a moment. "I have to leave now, but I'll text you and we can hang out tomorrow. Sound good?"

I nod, letting him kiss me one last time before he leaves the studio.

I'm happy that we finally finished our song, but I'm sad that we won't get to celebrate properly together in the moment. Karl's timing was pretty shit, but this is the lifestyle that we both live. Things like this are bound to happen.

I take out the flash drive with our song, and pop it into my purse.

Alex should be here soon, so I go to the break room to make a coffee. I set my purse on the couch, and take on the task of waiting for the world's slowest coffee machine.

Addison comes in and we chat a little bit, I tell her that Sebastian had to leave. She's bummed because she only got his text after coming all the way in. We chat for a bit, but then I join Tabitha at a table to have a good gossip.

Eventually, Alex and Hyacinth are ready to get to work. I grab my purse from the couch and join them.

***

After a long day at the studio, all I want to do is curl up on my couch. All the rest from the weekend still hasn't fully made up for how much I exerted myself. Sebastian says that's normal for a heat though, so I'm not too worried.

I order takeout and watch shitty reality TV for the evening. Although, I'm hardly watching it. Sebastian and I have been texting all evening. Texting is great and all, but I miss him more than that.

I feel so needy, but my couch isn't the same anymore. I wish he was here so I could snuggle up on his lap. This weekend was crazy, it's hard to believe that it's only been a few days since he kissed me. Everything has moved so quickly, and I'm finding it hard to navigate. It's so intense with him, and I don't know where we go from here. I'm scared to push him away, but I think my feelings are much stronger than they should be by now.

Plus, there's his human-hating family... What are they going to think about me? I mean, surely they have an opinion on it already, what with our already 'dating'. I'm guessing by the fact that he hasn't brought it up that it's probably bad. I want to talk to him about it, but is it too soon?

I switch off my TV, I'm not watching it anyway. I go to bed more confused than anything. But the one thing I do know is that I want to be with Sebastian, and that I will overcome whatever barriers we face.

***

I wake up with the sun shining through my window, it's warm and snuggly in my bed. I decide to spend the day writing, so I text Sebastian good morning and let him know I won't really be on my phone today.

Turning it to silent, I place my phone in my nightstand drawer.

My day is easygoing and relaxed. I eat delicious food and play around on my instruments, switching between my guitar and my piano. I even end up writing some things that I'm really proud of.

It's late in the day now and I should probably start thinking about dinner. I go and grab my phone to switch off a bit from the music. Opening my drawer, my phone is lit up with hundreds of notifications. What the hell?

I sit on the bed, crossing my legs and unlocking my phone. I open my main social media app, where most of the notifications are from. The home page shows a post from Sebastian, about the release of a new song.

He didn't mention anything about a new release... that's so weird. I click through the link to the Fortune Records app to listen to it. My heart stops when I hear the opening chords. I scroll down past the image and there it is, in black and white:

Home Again - Sebastian Orville feat. Flora

The phone falls to the floor, the song still playing quietly from it. How could he do this? We said we weren't going to release it, and what the hell is with the artist listing? This was my song to begin with!

I seethe, my breath coming quickly. We said that this was just for *us*. We wanted something that was separate from the label, something of our own. Did he lie to me?

I run through our time together in my mind. I thought I could trust him...

No, I can. I can trust Sebastian. He wouldn't break my trust like this. There has to be an explanation.

I pick my phone off the floor, pacing my bedroom while I check my texts. The one I sent this morning still sits in our chat, unread. I take a deep breath, trying to calm my heartbeat. I need to give him the benefit of the doubt, until he can explain himself.

Clicking through to his contact, I hit dial. It rings, and rings. I get put through to his voicemail.

"Hey Sebastian," I try to sound calm. "So listen, I saw that our song was released today... I thought we were clear with each other on not releasing it, but maybe there was a misunderstanding? I'm upset about it, so it would be good to talk. Can you call me back when you get this?"

I hang up.

Fuck, that was too nice, wasn't it? I don't want him to think I'm a pushover. But I also wanted to try and be understanding, getting angry wasn't going to solve anything.

I was going to order dinner, but my stomach turns at the thought of food right now. I sit on my couch and try to watch reality TV. My thoughts keep going back to Sebastian and the song. I force myself to wait a full hour before calling him again. By then it will be after 8 pm, he would definitely be finished working or due a break.

When the time comes, I try calling him. It rings out again, do I leave another voicemail? The beep sounds so I go ahead and say something.

"It's me again. I know you're working but I'm really upset about this, which I think is understandable. I just..." I sniffle, a few tears starting to pool in my eyes. "Nothing. Just call me please."

Fuck, now I am crying. I was doing so good until now.

I'm all alone in this, there's no one I can call. The label will still want me and Sebastian to play the happy couple,

I'm sure. So I can't talk to my friends and family about it. I can't talk to Rosie. Frank wouldn't be much use either, he'd only talk business, I've never really spoken to him about my feelings.

I start to sob, curling up and wrapping my arms around my knees. I didn't want to think that Sebastian was at fault here. But he's clearly avoiding me, which is stupid because we'll probably have to go on a date again soon. Unless he plans to get out of the dates... He could, he did tell me that he didn't care about the cause.

He's a self-admitted human hater! Fucking hell, he literally told me he didn't care. And did I listen? No, I went straight to his bed. I shiver as another sob takes my breath away. Maybe it was a bet? Was I a joke to him? Some game to play, how far can he trick a stupid human? I knew that it was all too good to be true.

I ring him again, giving him one last chance. His phone doesn't even fucking ring this time, going straight to voice-mail.

"You know what? I'm done being understanding about this. Clearly I was some sort of joke to you. Well, fuck you, Sebastian. I'm done. I'm done with this. I'm done with us. I'll speak to the label, get them to shut off this stupid PR shit. Or even better yet, maybe I'll get them to set me up with some other stupid fucking monster!"

I hang up, switching off my phone and tossing it on my dresser. Stripping off my clothes, I stomp into my bathroom. I turn on the shower and scrub myself, trying to get rid of any trace of Sebastian still lingering on me.

Sinking to the floor, I rest my head back against the tiles and let the water stream over me. I stay there until it becomes unbearably cold.

I barely dry myself off before getting into bed.

Chapter 28

My head is pounding, so I squeeze my eyes shut and try to go back to sleep. Crying all night does tend to leave you feeling hungover.

Wait, that's not my head, it's my door. Someone is banging on my door. I get up quickly and look for a weapon. Fuck, I don't have anything. If I'm quick, maybe I can grab a knife from the kitchen.

I creep down the hallway, my hands trembling. Maybe my neighbor finally enlisted help and decided to take some action. Just my fucking luck at the moment.

"Flora!" Sebastian's familiar deep voice calls. "I can smell you. I know you're there. *Please* open the door."

I'm relieved at first, but it's followed quickly by the sharp sting of betrayal. I stomp to the door, pausing with my hand on the handle.

"Please answer," he is quieter now. "Let me explain, Flora. *Please*."

Reluctantly, I open the door, but I leave the latch on.

"Keep it down," I hiss. "My neighbors already want me dead."

"I know, I know." He raises his hands, placatingly. "But I was worried. You weren't answering your phone. I called you from another number too and then you didn't answer that either."

"I'm surprised you care." I sniffle, unable to stop the tears that are flowing freely again.

"Oh, Flora." His eyes soften further. I look at him properly, and he looks a mess, his clothes and hair ruffled. He's red around the eyes too. "Please let me in, I'll explain everything. Please, let me look after you."

I shut the door in his face. Moving the latch off, I open it properly and step aside to let him through. Once he's inside, I shut it and quickly put the latch back in place.

Sebastian turns to face me, and I burst into a fresh torrent of tears. I pound on his chest with my fists.

"It was supposed to be *ours*!" I cry.

He wraps his arms around me and pulls me close to his chest. He leans forward and breathes in my hair. Picking me up, he moves into the living room, sitting on the couch with me in his lap. I cry into his chest, feeling an injustice in being upset by him but also needing him as my comfort. He shushes me, stroking my hair and rocking me back and forth.

Once my tears begin to fade, he starts to speak.

"I didn't release the song, Flora. I had nothing to do with it."

I hiccup, my tears drying up. I grab a tissue from the coffee table and wipe my nose.

"What happened then?" I ask, still clinging to him.

"It was Karl. He's not a good male, Flora. I'll explain everything, and give you the back story on Karl. But I can't stand how upset you are. Can I please look after you first?"

I've cried so much that I feel numb. So I just nod and let him care for me.

Sebastian potters around my kitchen before bringing me a cup of tea and a glass of water. I down the glass of water as he leaves again. This time, he comes back with the blanket from my bed. He tucks it around me, before snuggling up beside me. I rest my head on his shoulder and sip on my tea. I have to admit that this is all making me feel better.

He strokes my hair as he continues, telling me the full story.

"A long time ago, when I was first trying to make a name for myself in the industry, I met Karl. I was in the same stage of my career as you were when you met Frank. Karl was older than me, and he sold me the dream. I got drunk with him one night and he convinced me to sign a contract with him. Except I was young, stupid, and drunk enough to sign before reading.

"I didn't realize my mistake until the next day. You see, dragons hoard treasure by nature, and so we're usually one of the more wealthy monsters in society. My parents had done particularly well, and I never had to worry about anything. All it did was give me a false sense of my own worth. I thought I was invincible. A young, rich, strong and talented dragon."

I take a sip of my tea, resting my hand on Sebastian's thigh under the blanket.

"That's why I signed the contract. I didn't think there were any consequences for someone like me. Of course, there were. Karl practically owned me. He was taking an 80% cut of my earnings, and had full decision making rights over me as a person."

I grip his leg in shock. "Couldn't you buy yourself out of the contract? You said your parents were wealthy."

"They were," he sighs. "But not wealthy enough. The buyout on the contract was set at $10 billion."

"Holy shit," I whisper. "That's crazy! You'd never make that as an artist, no matter how well you did."

"I know," he hangs his head. "I've been stuck doing whatever the fuck Karl wants since then. Don't get me wrong, he's signed me to Fortune Records, and he's helped my career become what it is. But it's all self-serving, because his cut is so big. He also makes my life incredibly difficult.

"He's the reason I did the Noma shoot, and why I did our PR dating. So I guess some good did come out of it."

He kisses my forehead gently, a fond smile on his face as he looks at me.

"Once he realized that we were actually seeing each other, he was definitely pissed. I think it's why he called me out of the studio on Monday. He doesn't want me to be happy, Flora...

"He released the song behind my back and he kept me busy on set, hiding my phone from me. He released the song, barely giving you a feature, and I can't even do anything about it." Sebastian tugs on his hair, frustrated.

I instantly feel guilty, "I'm so sorry I jumped to conclusions. I was just so angry, and I—"

"Shh..." he strokes my hair. "Your reaction was completely valid. You didn't jump to a conclusion, you were trying to give me a chance at first."

I'm so sad for him, how he has spent his career being manipulated by Karl and forced to do everything.

"But, how did he even get the song?"

"I have no idea," Sebastian tells me.

There was only one copy, and it was on the flash drive in my purse. Setting my tea on the table, I slip off the blanket and check my purse.

"It's gone." I drop my purse on the floor. "He must have gotten it somehow."

I think back to when I was in the break room. I had left my purse on the couch unattended while I spoke to Addison and Tabitha. Anyone could have gone in it and taken the drive.

"I'm going to help you get out of this," I resolve. "I don't know how yet, but we're getting you out of this, Sebastian."

He looks at me with hope in his eyes. I will do it, I'm going to figure out a plan to get him out of this contract. I move back to the couch. Instead of slipping back under the blanket and snuggling him, I sit on his lap and straddle him.

My hands feel tiny around his face as they cup him.

"I'm going to help you," I kiss his forehead.

"But first," his nose next.

"I'm going to fuck you." I kiss his lips as I reach between us and unbutton his pants. I stroke his cock as I kiss him deeply, I try to put all my feelings for him into that kiss. When he's nice and hard for me, I sink down onto him.

We groan together as he fills me. I fuck him slowly, intimately, showing him my feelings through my kisses and how I move on him. My heart feels full as we look at each other, and I hold back the tears that are threatening to spill over.

After a while, Sebastian lifts me slightly and thrusts up into me. He keeps a slow pace, but he sets a hard thrust. I orgasm around him as he slips his knot inside me.

Curling against his chest, we wait out his knot in silence. Sebastian strokes my hair until I fall asleep in his lap.

Chapter 29

"Flora..." I burrow in deeper to Sebastian's warm chest, refusing to wake up. Even though my thighs burn from straddling him for so long.

"I promise you're going to want to see this."

His thumb strokes my lower back, where he has a grip on my ass cheek. I blink up at him, a frown on my face.

"You are so adorable when you wake up grumpy." Sebastian kisses my nose, before shoving his phone in my face. It takes me a second to focus on what's in front of me.

"What am I looking at?" I ask, leaning back and rubbing my eyes.

"It's the stats from our song. I know we didn't want it out there… but maybe we were wrong."

What? I take his phone from him and look at it properly.

"Holy shit…" I'm in awe. The numbers are through the roof. I switch to his browser, doing some searching.

"We're number one on all the charts," he answers my questions for me. "We've made history. The first song to ever be released featuring both a monster and a human."

I chew on my lip, a slow grin forming as I start to realize what this means. What this means for my career, too.

"Double the audience…" I think aloud.

"Exactly." Sebastian agrees. "People are listening to it, whether or not they support the cause. They're listening to it out of curiosity."

"Do you think they won't like it then..?" I ask, worried that we were going to be some sort of gimmick.

"No, sunshine. That's why they're listening to it in the first place, sure. But the reviews are good so far. People like it."

I squeal with joy, hopping up and dancing for joy. I'm sure that I look incredibly dorky, but Sebastian grins at me like I'm the light of his life.

"Now we can actually celebrate," he tells me. "It's 9 am, but I can order us breakfast and make mimosas."

I curl up in his lap again, unable to hide the massive grin on my face.

"You're the best!" I tell him, kissing him once before grabbing his phone to order food.

Chapter 30

"Are you paying attention, Flora?"

"Umm... yep!"

Liliana looks at me like she knows that's not true. A growl from Sebastian stops her from actually scolding me though.

Sebastian is currently leaning over me protectively, like I'm in any danger from the monster on the other end of the video call. I'm sitting on a bar stool in my kitchen, the laptop open in front of me on the kitchen island.

I'm getting mandatory PR training from the label. Apparently, Liliana is the best of the best. I was supposed to be doing the call on my own, and Sebastian was *supposed* to be waiting in my bedroom so I could have privacy.

Once he overheard Liliana reprimand me the first time though, he stomped into the room, demanding to speak with her. Our compromise? Him leaning over me like this while I tried to learn.

The problem was that I kept getting more and more distracted. He would breathe a little too heavily, the breath on my neck a tingle that went straight to my pussy. I'm a horny mess when he's this close to me. My body reacting to his warmth and the memories of how good he feels inside me...

"Flora!" Liliana snaps. "I'm done here. You've taken in whatever information you seem to be capable of. Sebastian, just do the talking for both of you. If you must speak, Flora, please try not to say anything that could get the label in trouble. We're toeing the line here, this is a tough situation to navigate and we *need* the image to represent the label's interests."

Shame drips down my neck, cold and slimy. I tear up a little, but I refuse to show her that she's gotten to me.

Sebastian stiffens, "Liliana. If you speak to Flora like that again, I'm getting you fired."

He exits the call before Liliana can respond.

"I'm going to do so bad," I sniffle.

"No you're not," he picks me up, holding me in his arms as I wrap my legs around him. "You're going to do great. I'll be there, and I will look after you."

We have an interview with the biggest monster radio station this evening. We're going to have to go into the station's studio, and there will be a performance of the song. Sebastian got the call with the invite pretty soon after we woke up.

So our day has been spent sitting on the floor of my spare room turned office. We practiced our song as we ate our breakfast, and even after. Sebastian kept the coffee coming and it was actually such a perfect morning. I needed to drink a lot of water and pop some painkillers though, feeling emotionally exhausted from the last twelve hours.

My phone dings and brings me back to the present, my lips moving against Sebastian's as he sets me down to sit on the counter. It's a text to let me know that wardrobe and makeup are here to get us ready.

***

The radio studio is pretty cool, memorabilia of different famous monster musicians covering the walls.

I'm asked to be the first human to sign their wall, and it's honestly such an honor. They ask me to place it next to Sebastian's signature, which he had done years ago. There's a photo op of us doing the signing, and then also of us getting a tour of the studio.

It really is a big deal that we're here together, presenting a unified front for humans and monsters. Our performance goes really well. I play piano, Sebastian is on guitar. Nereus, the drummer from Sebastian's band, joins us too. It's so fun to perform with them.

We're making our way into the sound booth now to meet with the DJ. He is a slim and handsome satyr male with a warm smile and a gentle handshake.

"I'm loving the song, you guys," he greets us as the recording of our single plays for the listeners at home. "Take your seats there and we'll start the interview once the song is over."

I move to sit in my chair, wringing my hands in my lap. Sebastian kisses my forehead gently.

"You're going to do great." He tells me, before sitting in his own seat.

"Welcome back to 98.7, where we play your favorite hits!" The DJ calls, and I quickly slip on my headphones, moving forward to the microphone. "I'm your host, Hedy, and I'm joined by two special guests.

"Monsters," he lowers his voice. "For the first time in 98.7 history, and the history of monster radio, we are joined by a human artist. Flora, our special guest, is joined by none other than our very own Sebastian Orville. The pair have been making appearances for the past few months, but yesterday they made history with the first song ever released by a monster and a human.

"Flora, can you tell us a little bit about what that felt like?"

I look at Sebastian, and he gives me an encouraging smile. Taking a deep breath, I answer, "Well, Sebastian and I both surprised ourselves by even writing the song in the first place! So to see it come to life like that and be received so well has been amazing."

"Incredible! And the credits for the production only lists the two of you. Was anyone else involved in the making of the track, or was it an intimate experience?"

"I have to say," Sebastian says, donning a charming chuckle. "The production was all Flora. I honestly can't take much credit for that, she's a machine when it comes to tech in a way I will never be. Trust me, I've tried!"

Blushing, I turn back to Hedy.

"To answer the rest of your question," I add. "We worked on it on our own. And we debated on whether or not we even wanted to release it. But in the end, we wanted people to know that humans and monsters can get along and create beautiful things together."

"That they can, it really is a beautiful piece." Hedy takes back control of the interview. "Can I ask you both a bit about your relationship?"

"That depends on what you want to know," I gently tease.

"Well, I think we were all surprised about how you two even met! Tell us about how you started dating."

"We met on the shoot with Noma," Sebastian takes this one. "I saw Flora and instantly knew that she was mine. She was, is, breathtaking, and I knew that I wanted to be with her. I was very lucky that we are both represented by Fortune Records, and I managed to get her number. It took a lot of convincing, but we spent some time together, deciding to go public quite quickly. But it was actually working on this song that truly showed me her beautiful spirit.

"I wish you could all witness her creative process, it's truly something to behold. I count myself lucky every day that she stays with me."

I gulp, Sebastian is looking me in the eyes with such an intensity. His eyes seeming to say that he means his words.

"How remarkable," Hedy says. "Well, we will all count ourselves lucky too, if you two keep making music like this.

"That's all the time we have today. Thank you for tuning into 98.7."

I slip off my headphones, trying my best to avoid jumping into Sebastian's arms.

***

"That was delicious," I say, licking my lips and setting my fork down on my plate.

Sebastian knocked it out of the park with dinner tonight. He said he wanted to cook something nice for me to celebrate our success.

"I'm glad you think so," he moves around to me, pulling my chair back and lifting me out of my seat.

I giggle as he shifts me and I'm draped in his arms, bridal style. My giggles turn into a moan though when he whispers in my ear.

"Are you going to be a good girl for me?"

"Yes, alpha." I say slowly and suggestively. He walks us up the stairs and lays me in his nest.

He unzips my dress and slips it down my body so I'm bared before him in my bra and panties. Those are removed pretty quickly, too.

I prop up my head and lazily tease my nipples as he strips off his own clothes. They're tossed to the side in a haphazard pile with my own.

"You're so fucking beautiful," he grunts the words, lifting me onto his lap. "Be a good girl and kiss your alpha like you mean it."

I groan, immersing my hands in his hair and pulling him down to meet me. I part his lips quickly with my tongue, letting it dart inside his mouth and explore. He takes over the kiss pretty quickly, unable to help himself from claiming me. I rub my pussy against his hard cock, the scales there teasing me into a frenzy.

Sebastian breaks our kiss, leaning back a little to look at me. "Flora?" his eyes search mine, breaking the scene a little.

"Yes, Sebastian?" I use his name to signal that I too am stepping back from our roles. I pause in my movement, giving him my attention.

"What's up?" I ask, when he remains silent.

"I love you."

My heart stops, a joy filling my chest. Three simple words and everything changes.

"I'm not sure when it happened, exactly." He continues. "But I wanted you to know, even if you don't feel the same way."

"I love you so much, you idiot." I chuckle, a few tears escaping my eyes.

Sebastian grins, cupping my face and swiping my tears away with his thumbs.

"I've been in love with you since before we kissed." I tell him. "I've been trying to play it cool. Didn't want to come on too strong, you know?"

We both laugh, clinging to one another. My heart is light and I feel like I'm floating.

"We're mates, Flora." He sighs, relief on his face as he tells me, like it's a big secret off his chest. "I smelled it when I first met you. I'm sorry that I didn't say anything. But at first I didn't want to believe it, and then I didn't want to scare you when I realized that you didn't know."

"Um.. Sebastian? I have no idea what you're talking about."

"Do humans not have *anything* sacred?!" He sighs, running his hand through his hair. "It means we're fated to be together. Everyone has a mate or mates, but that doesn't mean that they will ever meet them. You can love another monster and marry them, but mating comes above all that. Especially for shifters."

"So... we're destined to be together?" I tease, tickling his neck playfully.

"Yes." He says, very seriously. "It's why you went into heat too. You can only go into heat for your fated alpha."

"Oh." It would explain the strange pull I have always felt around him. Even at the fashion shoot when we met, I had felt it then too. No man had ever made me feel like that. It also probably explains why I always felt so strongly about him, even when that feeling was anger.

"There's something that dragon shifters do when they officially claim their fated mates. I'm not asking you to do it right now, I want you to understand the commitment properly before, if, you say yes."

"OK," I trust him, whatever it is. "What is it?"

"I would bite your neck, right here." He nips my neck with his teeth gently. "I'd have to shift a little to do it. Grow my fangs so I could pierce your skin."

He licks over the spot, before whispering directly into my ear.

"Then I would drink your blood, just a little. I'd knot you and claim you as mine, you'd tell me that you belong to me..."

My pussy is soaking, the image he is painting turning me on so much.

"Fuck, yes." I say, reaching down between us and fitting his cock inside me.

He groans as I move on him. "Not now, though. You need to think about it properly. Right now, you're going to be a good girl and take your alpha's knot."

Sebastian moves us so that I am laying on my back. He kisses me as he slowly thrusts his cock in and out of my pussy.

"I love you," he tells me as he picks up pace. "I love you so much, Flora."

His knot expands inside me and we cum together. He quickly turns us over, so that I'm draped over his chest.

Sebastian throws a blanket over us, kissing and cuddling me. He strokes my hair and tells me he loves me over and over as I orgasm on his knot.

Chapter 31

Sebastian and I received matching texts this morning to tell us that we needed to present ourselves for another PR date. This time at the studio for another artist's album launch party.

It was the perfect opportunity for us to enact our revenge against Karl. I'd been brainstorming the best plan of action the past couple days, and I had finally cracked it. Or at least I hoped I had.

My hair is parted down the middle, and I'm rocking my natural golden waves. I'm wearing the sexiest, skimpiest, little black dress that I own. My boobs are on full show, and the skirt barely covers my ass. I finished off the look with a simple gold chain that drapes long and disappears into my dress.

I arrive at the party. Alone.

I need to be alone for the plan to work properly.

Entering the space, I move to congratulate the celebrating artist. In my peripheral, I'm searching for Karl.

There he is, not too far from the bar, lurking in the corner on his own.

Karl is such an unfortunate looking male. And his current expressions aren't doing him any favors as he catches a glimpse of me. His gaunt, gray-skinned face contorts into confusion initially, the place where eyebrows would normally be drawing together.

His eyes scan the room, clearly searching for Sebastian. Who should be behaving perfectly, standing close and doting on me. I can see the moment that he realizes that I'm alone, his red eyes glowing in a fit of rage. He forcefully grabs his phone from his pocket, lifting it to his ear to make a call.

I speak to a few people, politely engaging in simple conversation, always keeping a watchful eye on Karl. I take a deep breath, I need to do this for Sebastian. With that, I meander over to Karl.

"Karl!" I greet him, holding out my hand. "It's so good to properly meet you, somewhere a bit more *comfortable*."

I lean forward a little, making sure that my boobs are in his line of sight.

"I'm sure you're wondering where Sebastian is," I make sure to fuel as much vitriol into his name as I can. "I told him not to come. He's *obsessed* with me, the poor thing. But, God, he's so weak willed.

"You know," I pat his chest as I speak. "When I was told I was going to get to date a real monster, I thought that would actually be the case. But he's not at all what I expected..."

I make sure to leave my hand resting on his chest a moment longer than appropriate. I can see the wheels in motion in Karl's mind. I really hope he takes the bait.

"I'm so *thirsty*..." I say, glancing towards the bar.

"Let's get you a drink then." He motions me to walk ahead of him.

When we reach the bar, he discreetly grabs my ass, squeezing tightly.

"I could show you a thing or two about how a *real* monster fucks..."

I give him a flirty smile, feeling so absolutely gross inside, as he orders our drinks. We sit at the bar as we quickly make our way through the drinks.

Once I see that he's finished his, I lean forward and place my hand on his bony thigh. I push my boobs together as I do, giving him my best bedroom eyes.

"It's kind of loud in here." I tell him. "I'm going to go somewhere quieter."

I don't wait for him to respond, slipping down off my stool and walking away. I feel him behind me as I walk down the hall, knowing that he's enjoying the feeling of stalking me.

I slip into one of the recording studios, leaving the door ajar. I hear the door click shut behind me as his gross, skinny tail wraps itself around my ankle, drawing me to a stop.

He moves close, his hands on my waist as he sniffs me.

"So you *have* fucked him..." he says.

I turn to look at him, hoping he doesn't try to kiss me.

"Yes, I fucked him. But then he became so obsessed with me, it was kind of embarrassing..."

He laughs, an evil glint in his eye.

"That checks out, Sebastian was always a bit too weak in that way." I place my hand on Karl's chest again, slowly stroking him. "But I did manage to take advantage of it, at least."

His words start to slow, slurring together. He doesn't seem to notice yet at least. I just have to hope that the bartender got the dosage of the muscle relaxant perfect.

"Can you fuck me like a real monster, Karl?"

"Of course, baby. I'll give you what he couldn't."

He leans in to kiss me and I turn my face to the side.

"I'm nervous though." I sigh. "What if you become obsessed with me like he did? What if you hurt me? I want to be fucked... but I don't want to die today."

Karl makes a frustrated sound, his breath coming in quick pants. He grips my ass and presses me against him.

"How about you ease my mind a little, first?"

He groans with impatience, "OK. What do you want me to do?"

I gesture behind me, to a sheet of paper, a pen laying next to it.

"Just sign this," I drag him forward, supporting some of his weight now that the drugs were starting to kick in. "It only says that you promise not to kill or maim me. Pretty standard stuff..."

He leans forward to look at the papers and I reach around him to palm his limp cock. The perfect distraction.

Karl quickly signs the papers with a flourish.

I move to the side as Sebastian steps in, having snuck in from his hiding spot in the sound booth. He grabs Karl around the waist, trapping his arms.

Snatching up the contract quickly, I follow our plan to the letter and get the fuck out of there.

Chapter 32

Mr. Chancey is broad like Sebastian, but he has much less muscle mass. He easily accepts the papers from me, his pale hands reaching across his desk to take them.

He is a dragon shifter like Sebastian, but Mr. Chancey's scales are the palest, ice blue in color.

"The funds have been wired." I tell him, my voice shaking slightly. "Do you need any proof of that?"

"No, child." He shakes his head, a gentle smile on his face. "I have been the lawyer for the Orville family for over thirty years. I know that they're good for it."

He is professional and courteous. Like any good lawyer, I guess.

"My discretion is assured." He flicks through the papers, making sure that the signature is there. "I will look after the rest."

It's a clear dismissal, so I head out of the office and take the elevator to the exit.

I really wish I had thought to change my outfit, but there wouldn't have been time anyway. It's not ideal to meet Sebastian's family lawyer dressed like *this*.

Mr. Chancey will be faking the notarization for Karl's signature. Sebastian was, hopefully, in the process of moving Karl to a discreet location so that he doesn't have an alibi for the evening.

Everyone at the party saw Karl and I have a conversation before leaving the party together. Our story will be that he came to the lawyers office with me to sign the contract. A story that Mr. Chancey was going to back up. Karl was going to see the error in his ways, signing away his rights to Sebastian's brand.

I make my way to the car. Surprisingly, Sebastian is waiting inside for me.

"You were supposed to meet me at your house," I scold him.

"I know, but I couldn't wait." I slip into his lap. "It was far too difficult to see his hands all over you, Flora. I could have killed him. I needed to be with you."

"You didn't hurt him though, did you?" I ask, a warning in my voice.

"No, I didn't leave a mark. I know that he needed to show no signs of coercion. It wouldn't have been worth it anyway, he lost consciousness right after you left."

"Everything worked out well on my end too." I tell him.

Sebastian runs a hand over his face, a rackety breath escaping him.

"It's all gone to plan," I continue. "You're free, Sebastian."

I shake him jokingly, joy filling me as his eyes light up.

"I don't know if I should be laughing or crying." In truth, he does both.

I lean forward, kissing his tears away one by one. Eventually, his tears dry up and I kiss him properly, my arms twining around his neck as we share our joy.

The car pulls to a stop and a glance out the window lets me know that we're home.

"I wanted to surprise you with something fun..." I say, my finger running down his chest.

Standing up as much as I can in the car, I slowly slip my dress off, displaying myself in my lace lingerie.

I reach behind me, opening the car door slightly.

"Give me a head start," I say, holding up the house keys that I stole from his pocket in my hand.

I turn and run towards the house, squealing with laughter.

Chapter 33

The cool, late night air makes my nipples stand up as I wait for Sebastian to find me. I ran as quickly as I could from the car, all the way up to the roof terrace.

Peeking over the railing, I can see that the car is gone. My heart speeds up even further as I think about how he is on the hunt now. I picked the roof for the drawn out anticipation, knowing that Sebastian would take the time to check every room in the house.

Deciding to bare myself completely for him, I quickly remove my lingerie. The anticipation is driving me wild, my pussy throbbing with heat. The longer he takes, the hornier I feel.

I want to touch myself so badly, but I want to save myself for him more. I want to be his good girl. My thighs are slick with my cum already at the thought.

When the door begins to open, I become aware of every part of myself. The tension builds as Sebastian comes out onto the roof, stalking me slowly. I stand very still before him, my hands by my side, as I wait to see what he will do.

He slowly walks towards me, then around and moving to stand behind me. Knowing that he's there and I can't see what he will do drives me wild. I feel his hot breath tingle against my ear before he speaks.

"Did you touch yourself?"

I'm so proud of myself for waiting now, knowing that I've done the right thing.

"No, alpha." I shake my head.

He nips at my ear. "Good girl."

I preen at his praise, a pulse of pleasure going through me. Sebastian's hand grips my throat and I relax into his hold.

His kisses begin at my shoulder, slowly making their way closer to my neck. Reaching down, he cups my pussy.

"Spread your legs."

I shift my feet wider and his hand moves easily against my wetness, rubbing my clit. I cry out, already so sensitive from waiting, and lean my head back against him.

"Fuck, you're so fucking wet." He keeps his movement on my clit a steady tease. "Are you my needy little prey? Waiting up here to be caught and fucked?"

"Yes, alpha." I whimper from the friction and his words.

"Good girl." His hand grips my throat tight, but not for long. Just a quick squeeze to show me that he can.

"Would you like me to bite you, my love?"

Holy shit, he wants to claim me, to mate me. Right now. Things have moved quickly, but I couldn't imagine my life with anyone else. I love this male, and I can't wait to begin building a life with him.

"Yes," I happily sigh.

"Do you know what it means for your alpha to bite you?" He pauses in his movements, making sure that my head is clear for my decision.

"Yes, alpha. We would be mated."

He chuckles. It's a sexy sound, but there is also pure joy in there too.

"Are you definitely sure that's what you want?"

Something sharp pricks where my shoulder meets my neck. He must have shifted into his fangs already.

"Yes, please."

He picks back up where he left off with my pussy, his fingers finding my clit again.

Sebastian's fangs pierce my skin, but there is no pain. Intense pleasure fills me, and the strongest orgasm forces its way through me. I collapse with its intensity, Sebastian catching me as he begins to drink my blood. Constant pleasure pulsates through my body with each pull.

After a moment, Sebastian retracts his fangs, his hot tongue slipping out to lap at my wound. I struggle to catch my breath, my head feeling light with the pleasure that has only begun to recede.

I stumble as Sebastian pulls away from me. I keep as still as I can, even though it is a struggle. He stands before me, still fully clothed in his suit from the party.

Sebastian unbuckles his belt and I immediately kneel before him, hoping he will let me lick his cock. I should probably wait for permission but I can't help myself. As soon as he slips himself free, my hands are on him, my tongue lapping at his head. I haven't had much opportunity to get my mouth on him, and I want to take my time and learn him properly.

Sebastian has other ideas though. Gripping my hair tightly, he pulls my face away. I keep my hands on his cock, stroking him as I look up into his glowing eyes.

"Open your mouth." I do as I'm told. "Stick out your tongue. That's it, good girl. You're doing so great for your alpha."

He moves forward and the tip of his cock enters my mouth. I groan as he pushes in, invading me.

"Hands behind your back." His voice has gone cold, a command in his tone that I can't refuse. "Now be a good girl and take what you're given."

He shoves my head forward, my lips stretching as I try to take him in. When he pulls me back to give me a breath, I try to relax my jaw wider, sticking my tongue out further.

The next time his cock enters my mouth, he forces me as far as I can go, holding me there. I wish I could take more of him, but I'm barely half way. I struggle to breath through my nose, my head feeling lighter. This time when he pulls out I cough, tears streaming down my face.

"Good girl." He reaches down to wipe my cheek. "You're doing so well."

Sebastian doesn't just hold in place now. He sets a steady pace, fucking my mouth with as much force as he can manage. Pleasure clouds his gaze and I'm happy, watching my alpha take his pleasure from me.

My vision starts to spot right before he lets me breathe again. I struggle to catch my breath, my chest heaving as I cough. But I feel so good. I smile up at him through heavy lids.

"Thank you, alpha."

I'm in his arms before I can blink. He flips me around and bends me over the railing. The only thing preventing me from falling to my death is his hand on my throat. I would be frightened, but I trust him completely.

"You've been such a good girl for your alpha." He bends over, speaking into my ear. "I'm going to claim you now, my love. Anyone who walks by will see it, anyone who is close enough will hear you scream for me."

I whimper at his promise. The thought of everyone being able to see him claim me fills me with such need. There's a hollow place inside me that I need my alpha to fill.

Sebastian pushes his cock into my wet, needy pussy and begins to thrust. I cry out as he takes me fast and hard. He wanted me to scream, and so I do. My moans fill the silent night, the only sound along with the slap of him against me.

I can feel my orgasm coming quickly, flowing over me and completely out of control. The drop below sends my adrenaline high, his firm grip on my throat grounding me at the same time.

"Who do you belong to?" Sebastian grunts, his voice the most animalistic I have ever heard it.

"I'm yours," he pounds into me harder than he ever has. "I belong to you."

Sebastian pulls me tight against him as his knot swells, sending me into another blissful orgasm.

Both of our breaths are coming quick, as he leans down and kisses his bite.

"You did beautifully, my mate." Oh, I like the sound of that word coming from him. His *mate*. "Stay still and I will try to pull out quickly. I want to look after you."

It takes a few minutes but he is able to pull out his cock, ever so slowly easing it out of me. Hot cum splashes out, the most I've seen from him.

Sebastian gently turns me around to face him. Wiping the tears from my cheeks, he kisses me so tenderly. I almost faint, my body giving up on me as the world spins. He picks me up in his arms and takes me inside.

Chapter 34

Everything I have ever done has led me to this moment. Seeing the wide smile on my mate's face as we leave the meeting room has made everything worth it.

Sebastian and I have just finished the most important meeting of both of our careers so far. We met with the head executives at Fortune Records.

Our first point of call was to negotiate a new contract for Sebastian, one where he is representing himself. With our single being such a hit, along with Sebastian's past success, we almost had exactly what we were looking for.

What sealed the deal was my sly reminder that my development deal was expiring soon. I casually mentioned that

I had my pick of recording labels to represent me with all the hype surrounding the success of the single.

We eventually settled, Sebastian and I both signing up for our next two solo albums. We were also going to be making some music together, with the label's full support.

I pull Sebastian into the bathroom, locking us into a stall for privacy.

"Shit… we really just did that…" I look up at my mate, seeing matching incredulity in his gaze.

"*You* really did that," he tells me, his hands on my waist. "You rocked it in there, I'm seriously impressed with how you handled that."

He bends, nuzzling my neck right by the mating mark. His new favorite thing to do since our mating bond was completed.

"Maybe I should have gotten you to be my manager." He chuckles, toying with my hair.

"Speaking of managers… how mad do you think Frank will be that I went behind his back?" I worry, fiddling with the lapel on Sebastian's blazer.

"Probably not at all when he realizes what his cut will be and that you did his job for him." Sebastian makes a sound of disapproval in my ear.

It wasn't the same with me and Frank like it was with Sebastian and Karl. I actually liked working with Frank, and

I wanted to keep doing so. Sebastian didn't like the idea of any man being close to me right now. It's apparently a bit of a side effect with the mating bond. Addison told me that it will fade with time though.

We met for coffee yesterday. Once Sebastian told her we had mated the night before, Addison insisted on meeting me for coffee. It was actually really nice to speak to her properly, and to hear all about her relationship drama.

"I'm so proud of you," I tell my mate, looking up at him.

"I love you so much, Flora."

Sebastian lifts me into his arms and kisses me. I lose myself in it for a moment, before remembering where we are.

"Ugh," I say, pulling away. "Can you please take me home so you can make out with me somewhere other than a bathroom stall."

Chapter 35

"I was super clear with my mom about not being early, but there's no promises there." I call to Sebastian, laying out the place mats on the dining table.

I'd recently moved my things to Sebastian's house. We were living here temporarily while we figured out where our forever home would be. Neither one of us really wanted to move out of our own places, but we did want to live together.

I mean, we were essentially even more serious than married. The mating bond being pretty much unbreakable.

Our compromise was to get a new place altogether. It made more sense for me to move in with Sebastian until then. Firstly, because my neighbors would have lost their shit if he moved in with me. Also, Sebastian could barely fit in my tiny apartment.

He was currently making pretty good use of the massive kitchen in this house, cooking up a storm for our dinner party. I was relegated to setting the table and making drinks. We both knew that having me in the kitchen would be a disaster. And we wanted to impress this evening.

I still hadn't met Sebastian's family, and the same for him with mine. So we decided to rip the band aid off all at once. Sebastian and I had yet to properly throw a party to celebrate our mating. We wanted to keep things private, so a home cooked meal sounded like the right move. We had a mix of family and our closest friends joining us this evening. Neither Sebastian or I have any siblings, but we were close enough with our friends that we wanted them to be there.

I finish my work in the dining room, heading back into the kitchen to pester Sebastian. Surprisingly, his parents were much more supportive than he thought they would be. They were initially furious when we were 'dating', but it turns out that our song was well received in their home. Once they realized that Sebastian wasn't about to make them social pariahs, they were more receptive. But when Sebastian told them that we were mated, his parents were thrilled. He had to hold them off on wanting to meet me properly until this evening. Mating bonds really were sacred with shifters.

My parents have always been so supportive of me. Although my mom freaked a little when she found out that I essentially married someone she hadn't even met.

Sebastian is making an array of different dishes, the kitchen counters covered with lots of different bowls and ingredients. He sat down yesterday with a notebook and properly planned out the timings for everything. It was adorable.

"Hey there," I wrap my arms around him from behind, snuggling into his back. "I've done all my things..."

My hands sneak under his apron, palming his cock through his trousers. I was insatiable when it came to my mate.

"Flora..." he warns.

When I don't let go, he sets his spoon down on the counter, turning to face me. His hand grips my throat as I continue to rub him.

"You know I have everything timed out perfectly. Now be a good girl and sit at the counter."

He had me there, I did want to do as I was told, after all. I let him kiss me softly and then take my spot, watching him move about the kitchen.

***

Dinner went better than I could have expected.

Sebastian's mother is elegant and poised, but she wrapped me in her arms as soon as she saw me, welcoming me to their family. His father was a bit more reserved, but still gave me a warm smile.

My dad was currently out in the garden with him, discussing politics over cigars and brandy. It turns out that all dads are the same at their core, monster or human.

My mom, on the other hand, doted on Sebastian. She did scold him pretty quickly on marrying her daughter before meeting her, but then softened when he told her that he would spend his life making me happy.

My current favorite dynamic was between Rosie and Sebastian. She teased him mercilessly, her sarcastic wit finally meeting a worthy opponent. Other than me, of course.

The rest of our friends were getting along. Daisy and Alex chatting with Addison, and Cleo hitting it off with both Nereus and Maddox. I met Maddox, the third member of Sebastian's band, for the first time this evening. The giant minotaur made even Sebastian look small, but he seemed like an absolute softie.

I watch our friends chatting, our mothers gossiping, and our fathers in the garden. It validates everything for me.

Back when I wasn't sure about whether or not to do the shoot with Noma, I had no idea that this would be in the cards.

Sebastian wraps his arms around my waist, holding a drink out for me. I take a sip, leaning back against him. monsters and humans really could get along. I hope that we can keep showing people that.

***

Waving goodbye to Rosie, our last straggler of the evening, I jokingly pat myself on the back.

"A job well done, I would say." I tell Sebastian, running my hands down his chest. We share a joyful moment, both relieved that the evening was a success.

He leans down, nuzzling my neck.

"Don't think I've forgotten that you misbehaved earlier…" he says into my ear. "You better find somewhere creative to hide this time."

I squeal as he smacks my ass, running away to be chased by my mate.

Epilogue

Six Months Later

I enter the rehearsal room where Sebastian is doing his thing with Maddox and Nereus. His shirt is slightly undone, sleeves rolled back as he rocks out on his guitar.

He looks so fucking sexy like that.

I sit in the back corner, watching as they finish up. I'm a bit early to meet him. OK, maybe I was early on purpose so I could watch a little.

My rehearsals finished up a few hours ago, so I got some groceries and took them home before coming back to pick up Sebastian.

The grocery list keeps getting more and more elaborate as Sebastian gets closer to having to eat out of a tour bus for eight months. I'm not complaining though. We're a couple weeks into rehearsals now, and we're going on tour next week.

Sebastian and I are going on tour together, with a double headline, both touring our new albums. I'm beyond grateful that we can do things like this, going on tour and making appearances together.

Once we were officially mated, Fortune Records held off on arranging any more dates for us. Which they didn't need to do anyway, since Sebastian and I were attached at the hip.

It didn't take long for us to find our new house either, or should I say for Sebastian to find it. He surprised me one day after being in the studio, picking me up to bring me home, except he didn't drive in the right direction at all.

Our house was a new building, in the up and coming area between humans and monsters, a suburb called Briar Hill. We were walking distance from the studio, and not far from Center Park, where we once had that awkward date. It turns out that if your human mate is amenable, a dragon shifter will go feral for chasing them in the woods. Quite literally. Sebastian and I have had quite a bit of fun with that.

With it being a new building though, the house had lacked character. But Sebastian knew that I would see the potential there.

He was right, I loved that I had a blank canvas to work with for decorating. I've been working with Nina, our interior designer these past couple months, so that the renovations on the house can be done while we're on tour.

I see that Sebastian is finishing up, and I can't help but make my way over to him. I kiss my mate in front of his coworkers, earning a few hoots and hollers. But I couldn't care less, I had my happy ending.

Want More..?

Sign up to the free tier on my Patreon to access a secret spicy bonus epilogue from *Snapdragon*!

And yes... there might even be shifted sex...

Sign up here:

A Note from Sofia

Thank you so much for deciding to pick up my book!

I write across the paranormal and omegaverse romance genres, please check out my other books if that interests you.

To stay in the loop, scan the QR code for my important links, or go to https://sofiaroseauthor.com/

To be updated of even more news, consider signing up to my newsletter on my website.

The Zodiac Society

If you enjoyed this book, try out some of my other stories... Month one is free on my Patreon.

Twelve signs. Twelve creatures. One challenge that could change everything.

When a freshman astronomy student stumbles into a nightclub that doesn't exist on any map, she's not looking for magic. She's looking for somewhere—anywhere—to disappear. But what she finds instead is a shimmering pocket of enchantment hidden on campus: the Zodiac Society.

By morning, she's waking up in Zodiac House with a choice—forget what she saw and go back to her ordinary life, or take the Zodiac Challenge: seduce twelve paranormals aligned with the signs of the zodiac, and earn her place in the Society. The rules are outrageous. The reward? Power, freedom, and a new name: Astraea.

Her first assignment? Aries.

Blaze is a faun with smoldering eyes, a sadistic streak, and a taste for control. His element is fire—and he knows exactly how to wield it. In a night of sharp pain and blistering pleasure, Astraea is stripped down, opened up, and set ablaze—inside and out. She's never submitted to anyone before. She never knew she could.

But this challenge is more than a string of pleasure-filled encounters. As Astraea dives into this world of monsters, magic, and illicit seduction, she begins to feel a pull toward something deeper—especially from the three Society members tasked with guiding her through the challenge: cool, clever Winslow; golden-hearted Ellis; and commanding, mysterious Miles.

And beneath it all, her body is changing. Her senses are sharpening. Something inside her is waking up.

Astraea might have entered the Zodiac Society by accident. But she's not leaving by choice.

ARIES is a high-heat, monster romance novella set in a secret society of pleasure, magic, and transformation. Each novella in The Zodiac Society series features a new zodiac-inspired creature, a spicy standalone seduction arc, and a slow-burning emotional journey that culminates in a shared HEA.

You will receive a new short story, exclusive art-work, and a page straight from Astraea's secret jour-nal every month!

Snapdragon

A human pop star. A grumpy dragon shifter. One fake relationship that's about to get very real...

Flora Augustine's career is on the line. With her development deal over and a new album on the horizon, she needs a miracle—or a monster.

Enter Sebastian Orville: legendary musician, dragon shifter, and a walking PR nightmare. When their record label merges the human and monster divisions, Sebastian is the perfect candidate for a fake dating stunt designed to bridge the divide—and Flora is the shiny new face of the campaign.

There's just one problem:

Sebastian doesn't like humans.

Especially not the kind he can't stop growling at.

Thrust into red carpets, steamy photo shoots, and far too much close proximity, Flora starts to wonder if the fire between them is more than just PR. But with knotting instincts rising and their reputations on the line, can they really fake it... without catching feelings?

If you love monster romance, possessive alphas, fake dating, and cozy settings with filthy heat, you'll devour Snapdragon.

Knotting • Heatplay • Celebrity Drama

Monster x Human tension

Omegaverse dynamics with a soft-spicy core

Start the Fortune Records Omegaverse series now - standalone romances, endless spice, and monstrous happily ever afters.